A SHORTNESS OF BREATH

a collection of little stories

D. B. Patterson

DBP Press 2015

A SHORTNESS OF BREATH

D. B. Patterson

DBP Press 2015

A SHORTNESS OF BREATH

Printed in the United States of America.
First Printing (eBook), 2014. Second Printing, 2015.

ISBN 978-0692420911

DBP PRESS
Post Office Box 399 | Tarpon Springs, FL 34688
Facebook.com/dbpatterson.author

For Tina.

AUTHOR'S
FOREWORD

A pair of friendly transients, a dead Santa Claus, a torn sack of presents, and an alley on Christmas Eve. An urban odd couple of religious zealots hopped up on cocaine and hellbent on revenge. Two lovers and a tearful final goodbye. A man's descent into hell and his attempt to save the woman he loves. A hurricane, an albino infant, a desperate country woman, a hoodoo midwife, a Grand Wizard of the KKK, and a man named Justice. A father still mourning the loss of his son spends the night on the Hollywood Walk of Fame when the Santa Ana winds blow. A post-apocalyptic world, a young man's lucid dream, and the doctor who falls for him.

And on the lighter side, a horrific wishing story.

That just about summarizes the short fiction collected here. I'm sure there's unifying theme, but I haven't figured it out.

A third of what I do when it comes to writing is purely instinctive, so pinpointing the specifics of why isn't so cut and dry. I often roll with certain decisions until a reason to do otherwise presents itself. The result here is less about an obvious cohesion and more about a study of moods. Yes, the genres and styles vary, but they do connect. Because I don't mind sharing sketches or interesting ideas, I've included a monologue from a stage play I'm currently writing PLUS a concept piece for a sci-fi novel I haven't finished.

By my standards, the quality of the work in this collection lies somewhere between not too bad and pretty good. Those published by magazines are labeled so. Those written and/or published for this collection also are labeled so.

—D. B. Patterson, December 2014

EPIGRAPH

A meeting in my mind took place

Where love and lust met face to face.

Assembly in my upper room

Concealed in snake-like coils, my womb.

My thoughts had lingered close to see

A violent contest fought in me.

For lust had raged and craved love's blood;

Love had vied for a fiery flood.

But they desisted, ceased to talk;

Around each other they did walk.

There was no struggle nor a fight.

The two opposing lost their might.

Why should they scream their battle cries,

One winning where the other dies?

They both must live, they must forgive.

For lust is love, drained from a sieve.

—D. B. Patterson

Santas, Sweetly

Written exclusively for this collection.

Professor stops in near-pitch shadows. His hands are eyes that read the freezing alley wall—cold bricks, garbage dumpsters, a phalanx of aluminum trash cans where rats roam and plot. Wafting into the alley from a nearby street-corner, a jazz medley of 'Up On The Housetop' and 'Jingle Bells'.

There's also the stench of urine and feces, rotting fruit and unseen refuse, the effluvia of city life. And just over there is a dead man who fell out of the bleak winter sky.

A week later, and no one's looked for him.

Not here, Professor thinks with a smile. He creeps along

the wall. Sings of reindeer and stockings for Little Will and Nell. Steps over crates and broken boxes. Pauses where the fallen man had raised such a clatter. Turns his gaze upward.

"Poor Kris Kringle," Professor says.

He dropped from the rooftop, you see—from way up there between those two tall buildings.

He fell through the clotheslines crisscrossing the alley. He fell past the brown spider plants and their frozen spindly legs. Fell past Mrs. Wilson's window boxes of faded plastic poppies, all staring ahead mouths-agape like a silent choir of old pink vulvae. Past the dead Creeping Charley vines buried in the bricks below the busted fire escape.

There.

He landed there, right under that twisted iron ladder in a heap of bloody broken Christmas.

Here, in crimson coat and cap, his arms and legs akimbo, lies Santa Claus. Dark stain congealed beneath his comically flattened head. White beard caked with vomit. Silver belt buckle smeared with blood. Charcoal mittens streaked with cake icing. And spilling from his ripped sack are dozens of little blue boxes topped with tiny white bows.

"Click, click, click," Professor hums. "Down came Old Saint Nick."

Police sirens whine between horn blasts of passing fire trucks. The roar startles an old woman snoring in a milk crate on the concrete. But Virginia, a decayed hag who calls herself Thumbelina, is too wrapped in a lovely ripple buzz to care. She adjusts her wine bottle pillow and goes back to sleep, oblivious to all noises.

With a grin, Professor slips under a plumbing pipe. He plugs a plastic Baby Jesus head into the wall outlet hidden there. Bathed in aqua light, he kneels at the grave of the festively bloated dead man. Hearing angels in a water drain, he clasps his hands together.

"Calling all falling Fathers Christmas," Professor prays. "Come drop from the rooftops, come lay down your sweet heads—click, click, click—calling all Clauses and Kringles. O, come, all ye Santas, sweetly sleep with us on this rancid Feast of Stephen. Lord Jesus, this was your jolly sacred elf, and we do give thanks for the bounty in his sack. Amen."

Then come muffled meows.

Professor laughs as four kittens pop fuzzy heads from

under the red and white cap. They tumble down in search for his coat pocket kibble. It's hide-n-seek until all fall into a pile of fur, licking, and paddy-paw biscuit-making.

Petting them, he shudders.

Cold air tickles his stubborn need to feed his very bruised arms. Well traveled vein tracks are little mouths hungering for sugar plumb fairy milk.

Yes, the miracle elixir for dreaming of candy canes instead of holiday corpses. But without a needle, Professor must ignore the itch, the constant itch.

He lights a cigarette and takes long drag. "This'll have to do for now," he whispers. Taking a swig from his bottle of rotgut, he gently plays with the kittens and blows smoke rings into a cold sky of bitter stars, and...

CRASH.

Thumbelina has thrown her pillow.

The silent night suddenly shattered, Professor grimaces. The kittens claw him as they scatter in fright. He drops the burning end of his cigarette on his ankle. And he nearly loses the grip of his bottle when the old woman plops beside him. She rests a matted head on his shoulder of faded, filthy hounds-tooth and gazes at her sparkling fingers. She smiles a toothless smile as she counts each ill-fitting diamond ring.

Street-jazz 'Drummer Boy' rolls into 'Greensleeves'.

Professor scratches himself. "The perfect soundtrack for more gift-giving," he says, planting a blue and white box on the old woman's knee. Tapping her arm, he says, "Merry Christmas, Virginia, my dear."

She drops her gaze. "My, my, my—for me? Another gift?"

"Well, you've been such a good girl this year."

"Hush your mouth. I've always been on his naughty list."

Professor chuckles. "Not this year, Virginia, my dear—well, open it."

She opens the lid. Sudden tears make muddy tracks down her cheeks as she slides a new platinum band onto a bony thumb. "The sack is far from empty, Virginia," Professor says, putting an arm around her. "A blue Tiffany box each day to make up for all the years Santa screwed you."

"That's a whole life of years," she says, admiring her fingers despite the all the grime. "I'll look like an empress by then. Will you say something Shakespeare now? It's my favorite part of the gift-giving. And I like it when you call me Thumbelina."

Giving her a squeeze, Professor decks his lap with kittens upon their return. He digs up an old memory and rehearses its words in silence.

"Here's something Shakespeare for my Thumbelina," he says, adding, "from *Hamlet*. 'Some say that season wherein our Savior's birth is celebrated, they say no spirit dare stir abroad, no planets strike, no fairy takes, nor witch hath power to charm—so hallowed, and so gracious, is that time.'"

Thumbelina quietly claps, her rings jing-ting-tingling. "Professor, let's drink to Hamlet and Santa Claus and Big Baby Jesus Head—the little blue shit's gonna be born again soon."

Professor passes the bottle. "It's midnight," he says with a sigh. "Shining as a new Bethlehem star, the moon gives the luster of midday to us objects below." After placing a finger to his lips, he tucks the sleepy kittens away in the dead Santa cap manger for a long winter's nap. "If only the stars weren't so merry and bright," he says. "If only they'd stop screaming."

"Screaming stars?"

"Yes, Virginia, screaming in heavenly peace."

*

Other Roads to Damascus

Originally published by *Larks Fiction Magazine*.

And so it came to pass that Saul was baptized in the unisex restroom at the Midtown Atlanta MARTA subway station.

Black Rudy, Junkie Prophet of the Homeless, cupped the white man's face with chocolate hands. There, three crosses to the forehead, three splashes from the sink, three shouts of praise, and three lines of holy blow—Father, Son, Holy Ghost.

A triple-dipped sacrament before the final judgment of a wicked man. Today was a time to kill.

Amen, amen, amen.

Jacked-up on Leviticus and coke, Black Rudy and Saul left their reliquary and fell into the crowd flow.

They watched silver subway tubes spilling, filling, and fleeing with passengers. Across the tunnel face above the late afternoon workday circus loomed granite slabs, each a totalitarian-themed bas-relief. Beaming rays of a glorious communist sun, happy Marxist farmers, their wives and children—joyful socialists of an unseen collective.

There was music on the Ashford/Dunwoody line, an urban symphony of people moving as one, of brakes screeching in cacophonic melodies across the platforms, of urchins who played jazz for pocket change. An escalator moved Saul and Black Rudy, ivory orphan and ebony preacher, to the surface and a parking lot of cloud-white buses.

They boarded the #23, northbound from Atlanta to Marietta, and waited ten more minutes before the coach finally departed. Being only half-full, several people from the back moved to open seats up front. The duo remained seated in the very back. Side by side and ever fidgety as they nodded to each other and spoke in furious whispers.

Saul, breathless and sharp, said, "There's a time to every purpose under heaven, and it's a time to kill the wicked."

In Caribbean and Deep South tones, Black Rudy muttered bible passages and musings from his own brain— manic rants found only between the bookends of three-day benders. "God-Daddy never passes arbitrary judgments," he said. "And Old River Chaos tests us 'cause we can't know God-Daddy's mind. You shut de fuck up when dat still-soft voice comes and tells you to do His will, an' dat's de only purpose you need to know."

Amen, amen, amen.

Saul was staring at his hands, instruments for the righteous act of judgment. His chest was a warren of mad rabbits digging holes until the emptiness summoned visions. He imagined what he'd do to the man they were going to see. The man living north of the Kennesaw sticks.

And Saul pictured squeezing the doomed man's neck, hands under a fleshy chin and doughy red face, the helpless man clawing at them as the light of wide green eyes faded to shades of dusty, empty hazel.

Legs dancing in little jigs, Black Rudy said, "If'n you got

blessings to count, best do it 'fore God-Daddy trows down a bolt from up in Heaven. We 'bout to walk de earth like His baby-boy, an' He won't like it if we fuck shit up."

Thump-thump, thump-thump.

Saul, grinding his teeth, said, "Amen, amen, amen."

Black Rudy, his mane of dread-beads clicking, nodded.

As Fulton County's rush hour traffic headed for Cobb County, Saul forgot his hands and counted blessings.

He closed his eyes and remembered.

Losing all—sanity, home, job, friends—a great fall that presaged a shattering that preceded a rising from destitution. A Junkie Prophet and his congregation of urban nomads, monks working subway crowds, earning money for spirits and coke to better understand a new testament and to master its two great secrets.

One, that a breathing hand opened empty but closed full, and two, that a life in the street was freedom, the greatest blessing, and a reclamation of Eden.

Thump-thump, thump-thump.

The sea of barely moving vehicles on the I-75 corridor meant at least an hour of air-conditioning.

Filled with gratitude, Saul and Black Rudy waited with grins as the bus crept across what once had been the Chattahoochee River. Months of drought had scorched banks into caked clay, cut by a thin trickle and flanked by sentinels of bony Georgia pine.

And so it came to pass that the #23 unloaded two passengers into the hot, encroaching twilight.

The air was bayou-thick, and a boiling sunset walk to Acworth was fast-becoming a crawl. As luck would have it, a flatbed truck ride took them to the woods surrounding what was left of Lake Altoona.

And there, they followed a dirt road southeast around the marshes of the southern shore.

Leaving the main road for a narrow path, they headed west until the anorexic trees revealed a clearing. Saul pointed to the silhouette of a farmhouse on the distant hill. "There, a quarter-of-a-mile ahead," he said, suddenly searching the ground around his feet.

"What is it, boy?" Black Rudy asked.

"A well used to be here somewhere, forty-feet below with a thick wall, a bucket and pulley—my uncle must've covered it up, the bastard."

Black Rudy kicked dust clouds as he sat on a fat stump. He hummed the melody of a Negro spiritual, dug inside the front pocket of his trousers and pulled out a bottle of water for Saul and a second for himself. He drank as he cut the holy blow, three lines apiece laid out in tangents to the stump's tree rings.

"Let's jack-up for God-Daddy 'fore we go to your uncle's house for his judgment," he said. "Tirteen months o'no damn rain points to demon trouble, Saul-baby, so I hope you see tru pitch. Now, come over for my blessing and talk 'bout what's to happ'n up'n here."

Saul did as he was told.

The Junkie Prophet cupped his disciple's face. Three forehead crosses smeared with spit, three shouts of praise, and then three lines.

Father, Son, Holy Ghost—amen, amen, amen.

Sitting on the grassy edge, Saul sipped water and studied the parched ground, starved for moisture. It must have siphoned fluid from the poor Kudzu, turning green leaves and fat vines into brittle yellow twine.

Blackberry brambles fared only slightly better and bore runt fruit between leaves caked with clay dust. A once lush place of flowers, vegetable gardens and peach orchards was now white-washed and dying.

Somewhere around here was the deep well—had it dried up? Its wall of river stones lay about in broken piles that marked nothing.

Where is the fucking well?

Childhood landmarks had vanished, turning Saul's memory backwards. A warm wind carried a familiar scent of ripening peaches, hinting at something familiar until he felt lost again.

Still, somewhere here was the well he'd spent ten long years braced against, wishing with pebbles as coins. It was a place for finding courage to face long nights paralyzed in his bed, waiting for Uncle Bud to find him.

"Everything has a season," Saul said.

"And a time to all heavenly purposes," Black Rudy added. "I see changes in destiny comin', mine and yours. You got de damned sight, boy, so I know you seen changes too—reason 'nuff to call you by name!"

"My name?"

"Dat's de path of your destiny," Black Rudy chimed.

Saul's people were Kennesaw Mountain crackers, rural folk deeply entrenched in religion, superstition, and moonshine. Aunt Tilly was his mother's sister. She'd once told him about his mother's lifetime of bible-reading. It was something she did every day until the car wreck that took her and his father. Names like Enoch, Saul, or Micah were as ordinary to his parents as Bob, Joe, or Billy.

How is Saul *my destiny?*

Black Rudy put hands on the young man's head. He shouted a prayer and shook in an Old-Testament Rasta-frenzy. He spun in a whirl of dancing and shuffling. He lifted his arms to the setting sun and howled.

"God-Daddy, give dis gentile strength to kill an evil man t'nite. If'n killin' ain't your will, I pray dat You give us a sign before he shoves a smitin' flamin' angel sword up'n dat uncle's unholy ass. I know dat You got some plans cooking even for all de ugliest of Your motherfucking uglies."

"Amen, amen, amen," said Saul.

The farmhouse now cast longer shadows, each a dark

bone-finger penetrating the soft places of the surrounding forest. They waited for a sign as twilight gave way to a rising moon. Black Rudy leaped in a chicken dance, grabbed Saul's hands, and pulled them towards the house.

Thump-thump...

There, now only a hundred yards before smiting a very wicked man. There, only seventy-five yards before drinking ice water and taking a shower and eating a stolen supper of fresh vegetables and steak. Forty-five yards before sleeping in a real bed, before a blessed blackout and a late breakfast.

Twenty yards.

...thump-thump...

Eight yards.

...thump-thump.

They reached the farmhouse.

Candlelight glowed in one of its windows. Beneath it, they climbed two upended metal crates and peered inside a tiny bedroom. Lying on the bed against the opposite wall was a woman, Saul's Aunt Tilly.

Draped across her forehead was a cloth. Her face was bone-thin, wrinkled, fever-flushed, and sweat-stained.

Clutching her hand was Uncle Bud, smaller, thinner, old. Beside her, he rocked in prayer, wiping her face and weeping as she howled in pain.

"Black Rudy, that's him," Saul began, "but—"

—but he couldn't finish.

Aunt Tilly sat upright and screamed obscenities. Uncle Bud held her down until the fit passed. He wiped away vomit and mucus, mopped the drool and blood, and after she was still for several long moments, the cycle of fits and vomiting repeated.

"You sure dat's de wicked man, boy?"

Wiping his face, Saul nodded.

Laughing, Black Rudy sat on the crate, his back against the wall. "Dat man in dere," he said, "is tendin' to a woman doin' battle wit de devil, an' he might'a raped you back in de day, but he ain't now. He's in hell if'n ever I seen it, an' dat's a truth to kick de shit outta you."

Saul studied his uncle and dying aunt for as long as he could stand it. A life of poison began to drain from his body. He sat beside Black Rudy and said, "The man I knew as a child doesn't exist. I can't take the life in there."

Amen, amen, amen.

"Can't tell what God-Daddy wants," said Black Rudy, still laughing, "but killing ain't it. Sometimes, you gotta take other roads to Damascus. Now let's get cleaned and steal us some fruit before we head back."

The two men stripped off their dirty clothes as the night air filled with scents of peach and honeysuckle. They ran to the orchard and drank from a nearby garden hose, refilling their bottles and spraying each other like pagan boys under the bright moon light.

Dancing away from the trees, they sat on a stone fence to watch fireflies and bats. They listened to the crickets and tree frogs and gorged themselves on handfuls of stolen peaches.

After a final wash-up, they dressed and headed back.

"How you feel, boy?" Black Rudy asked.

Saul smiled. "God-Daddy is great—amen, amen, amen."

At the clearing, they discussed camping there as they passed over its center. Midway, a sound like muffled thunder sent a pair of muskrats scurrying from a patch of nearby cattails. The two men stopped mid-stride when a thicker crack heralded four ripping creaks.

"What was that?"

A handful of moments passed.

"Black Rudy, what was that?"

"Shut-up, boy," the Junkie Prophet said, spreading his arms wide like a bird. "God-Daddy is great—amen, amen, amen. He's speakin' to you, boy, so git ready to witness Him a miracle. I'm de Holy Ferryman."

Four more cracks, like shots from a cap gun.

Black Rudy raised his arms toward the sky. "What a friend we have in Jesus. All de sin an' grief to bear! What a privilege to carry ever-y-ting to God in prayer! Fuck dis sinner, Heavenly Daddy!"

Thump-thump.

A final piercing crack.

A gaping mouth opening beneath their unsteady feet. Of the two men standing there, only one fell. As if the earth decided to quench its thirst by swallowing the man whole, Saul fell.

All the way down, Saul counted heartbeats.

Thump-thump.

Time slowed as he dropped like a stone through the stale weightless air. He waited for the bottom. A slope caught his body, breaking the fall through all that cold blackness.

Thump-thump.

Saul opened his eyes.

He didn't remember hitting bottom, but there he was with muddy water up to his waist. And the smells of damp soil and rocks, the sounds of spiders and centipedes, the dusty spray of pebbles and debris.

Thump-thump.

Saul closed his eyes.

His memories were disjointed recollections. Loose boards and cracks, a slow drop into the heart of this god-damn deep thing, and then nothing else afterward. Sensations of flying sent a rush of chills across his flesh, stippled goose bumps burning briars into his arms.

Not much pain, but breathing was not easy.

And he tasted metal.

"Amen, amen and amen, boy!"

Thump-thump.

Saul opened his eyes. He winced as he sat upright in the

muck. Black Rudy shouted into the well.

"Once dere was another Saul who slaughtered disciples an' journeyed near to Damascus," the Junkie Prophet said, his voice echoing. "Light from heaven bitched-slapped him to de earth as God-Daddy struck de man fool-blind for sins 'gainst de Holy Son. After repentin', Saul saw notin' an' nobody for days. Man had no sight, no food, no drink— God-Daddy jacked his ass up in a fit of blindness."

"God-Daddy jacked your ass up too, didn't He?"

A long stretch of silence followed before Black Rudy added, "Answer me, white boy! What do you see now?"

Saul managed a loud grunt. "Fuck you, Black Rudy!"

"Don't you holla at me like I'm a nigga," the man replied with a chuckle, voice trembling in the euphoria of sleep deprivation and too much blow. "God-Daddy be praised! Amen, amen, amen! I'll go'n git you some hep at de farm-house. Won't be long, no way, no how, but if'n you die a bit 'fore I come back here, you best forgive your uncle, hear me? Demons abide in all us fool sinners, ev'ry goddamn one of us. Have we trials an' temptations? Don't be discouraged— take it to de Lord in prayer, boy."

Then, Black Rudy left.

Thump-thump.

Saul closed his eyes.

Alone and cold, he counted his tick-tock heartbeats to pass the time.

He counted blessings ever time he moved a finger or a toe. He counted the pain each time he breathed a breath. Yes, time, time, time that whittled at him, nip-nip-nipped at his mind as he teetered on the razor sharp seam of wakefulness, and oh did the lucid phantoms come for him.

Sounds—singing, laughter, applause.

Scents and taste—baking bread, chocolate-chip cookies, hot buttermilk biscuits, nutmeg. Sights—Mama's moon face full of yes-baby love, a beach of sugar white sand on the bottom of his wet feet, flocks of pink flamingos. And touch, yes—the tickle of ladybugs, cold running water, fresh cow manure between bare toes.

Leaving that strange lucidity, he began to drift. Saul recalled the story of a coked-out homeless idiot who fell into a well after following a profane schizophrenic Rastafarian monk through the dry Georgia wilderness.

Amen, amen, amen.

He recalled a dream he had about a boy who loved to fish. The boy would row his red boat to a secret place where fish hid on sunless days.

There were schools of bream there always, and by day's end his catch trailed in the water behind the boat as he paddled back to the dock. He'd unload the tackle and tuck the boat into a shed near an old well.

Sitting against its mossy wall, he'd breathe deep the dampness as he imagined living in its depths until God transformed him into something else, something altogether different than himself.

For there is a time to every heavenly purpose.

Thump-thump.

Saul opened his eyes.

He smiled when one of Black Rudy's vulgar sermons popped into his head. His homeless guru was somewhere up there, his voice blending into several others that shouted down to him.

Only one voice cut through the clamor.

It belonged to a woman who kept asking him to say

his name, please-please-please she kept asking him again and again to just say his name. A sudden roar and thumping overpowered her sweet sounds. Oh, but the voice returned—yes it did, yes it did.

Again, the woman asked the same question, which fell around his broken body in as many pieces. A name—yes, the woman asked for a name.

And so it came to pass that he finally spoke to the darkness.

"My name is Paul."

Thump-thump.

"Paul," came her reply. "Hold on, Paul."

Paul.

He said it aloud again. Before the return of roaring thunder and heart thumping, he said it again. He repeated it, reveling in the sound of it. As an unseen bed slipped under him and pulled him from the water, he said it again.

And rising up into the morning air, he said it as muddy blood sloughed from his skin.

He said his new name and smiled.

Thump-thump.

Paul opened his eyes.

He wasn't surprised that he couldn't see anything yet. Blinding blurry light amidst the white noise of whirring machines and crowds of people—yes, he expected that much. And there was a so much light up there waiting for him. Only a voice. "Hang tight, Paul," it told him.

Thump-thump.

Paul closed his eyes.

Whether his eyes were open or closed didn't matter now anyway. God took his sight down in the darkness. God would return it here on the surface when He was ready for him to see.

"Almost home, Paul."

Thump-thump.

In the cacophony of everything happening around him, there was only a single chord of music, the sound of a woman's voice. She kept his heart beating as he left the black bowels of the earth. She kept Black Rudy at bay as his rescuers hoisted him safely from the hole.

Not even the Junkie Prophet could drown the sound of that woman's voice, not even with all his cuckoo crooning and vulgar proselytizing. Not this woman's voice.

"Paul, you're safe," she told him. "Open your eyes."

As strange hands poked and prodded his bruised, blood-ied, and battered body, he began to wonder if she was just a dream. Then he heard it again, her voice.

"Paul, open your eyes for me."

Louder and closer, he heard it again.

"Paul, I know you can hear me," she said, taking his hand. "You have a smile on your face, Paul. Open your eyes."

He squeezed the fingers grasping his.

Thump-thump.

And knowing that he'd never again hear her speak to him again, knowing she'd shine a penlight in his pupils and summon Black Rudy to take her place, knowing it would herald the final moments he'd spend with this angel—he opened his eyes.

Turning his head, he looked at her face with a smile. It hurt to look at her joy.

Thump-thump.

"Tell me your name," he asked, blinking back tears.

"My name is Mary," she said, smiling as she wiped his

forehead and face with a cloth. "It's nice to meet you, Paul."

He began to weep. Her face was a blinding sun, and it hurt to look at it, but he saw clearly now.

After all, his was the name of a saint.

Amen, amen, amen.

*

D. B. Patterson

Eurydice Rising

Published exclusively for this collection.

Cigarette hangs loose, dangling drugstore dangerous.

Match burns in slow motion ragtime as it finds the flame. A moment of anticipation, a sweet too-quick inhale in the last seconds before relief floods him, as a breaking levee in his lungs.

Ah, yes, the breathing orgasm.

He smokes against a brick wall.

Waiting there, an ancient gym bag over his shoulder, he glances at his watch, the diving one that glows underwater.

He looks up into a misty gray sky. Drops his gaze to

puddles of tainted rainwater pooling in the parking lot. Breathes cold air burdened with smells of cooking grease, motor oil, and fresh asphalt fuming in scents of Ben Gay and gasoline.

The young woman moving toward him opens the door to his left. Flicking away his half-smoked fag, he follows her downstairs into bright lights, warmth, and waves of techno music. Tempo a sexy cardiac arrest—*pump, pump, pump, pump*—pounding his temples.

Clanging metal plates, whirring treadmills, televisions, ambient conversations, bodies in motion. He hangs back to watch the woman approach the front desk.

Deskman smiles at her.

She glances sideways, picks up a pen, and removes strands of hair from her mouth. Scribbles on a clipboard and then motions to the hanging tanning sign over a curtained entrance. Winks a slightly dazed blink and disappears into the back rooms—*pump, pump, pump, pump.*

The watcher waits. He walks over to the desk and signs the space under her signature. Touches scripted letters, elegant curves traced with a finger. Reads his name with hers and chuckles at the odd pairing. Imagines her face and re-members her hands, phantoms over his body and heart—and yes, goddammit, he knows he's wasting time.

"How you doing there, Onyx?" Deskman asks.

Pump, pump, pump, pump.

Someone drops a plate in free-weights. Someone opens a door and lets out aerobics instructions on crackling loud-speakers. Someone cranks up the heart attack music. Desk-man speaks again. "Onyx?"

"Oh, protein bar, please—I'm fine, you?"

Deskman, sliding the bar and shrugging. "Two dol-lars—no complaints, and I haven't seen you in what, six or seven months."

A statement and a question.

What's his fucking name? Rudy, Roger, Roy, Raymond—dammit, Deskman will have to effing do.

Onyx lies. "Long gig up in New York."

"Modeling?"

"Something like that," Onyx replies. He takes a few in-terval moments to think. Swallows shy edges and chews his lip. Hands move through jet-black hair, spider fingers feeling his face and reading his chin stubble. Sees where the young woman went—the tanning beds—yes, back there.

Despite everything, all is right with the world simply because she's there. Deskman, grinning and pandering. "Go on back there, man—she's in thirteen, and take your time—it's dead today."

Onyx, nodding. "Unlucky thirteen."

Invisible chains pull him through the curtains. Walking deliberately, Onyx rakes painted concrete walls. Inches past rising odd numbers and stops at a blue door, its rust-red thirteen hanging in a backwards split.

Rap-tapping, he enters the room and closes the door. Inside is a blinding bed doused in black-light with honeybees rumbling beneath it.

The young woman is waiting on a white plastic lawn chair. Clad in white panties, she crosses her legs and pulls pink goggles from her eyes. Blonde hair, tiny hands, little feet, bronzed skin with a freesia scent—the kind that lingers after she leaves a room.

"Hi, Onyx."

"Hi, Billie—it's good to see you."

Pump, pump, pump, pump.

Billie grips her chair. His voice shifts her senses. Makes her see stars that blind her. Makes her hear music that deafens her. Makes her feel places in her heart she thought long dead. His voice opens shut things not meant for everyday sight—it unhinges her.

Pump, pump, pump, pump.

Billie swallows her joy—she can't show it. She ingests it, which is agony, as the pill she popped in the parking lot begins to tickle her mind into a delicious white noise. "Come kiss me," she says, arms open.

"I don't think so," Onyx says, arms crossed and fingers clenched. He knows her pills, knows this one helps her forget pain.

"Why, baby?"

"Because you're on something."

Billie hands him her bed goggles. "Don't burn your baby blues into reds. Cameras don't lie, baby—not even for you."

"What are you going to do?"

"I'm gonna sit here while you bake your honey buns," Billie says. "I'm always on something, Onyx. After tonight, you'll always be on something if you want to play Gregor's game."

Onyx locks the door. "I know his game"

Billie giggles. "The hell you do—things have been different since your noble escape left me bereft of a soul."

"I was trying to save us—to get you out of there."

"Well, don't try to save me ever again," Billie says. "I got in this business because it pays well. Because I'm nothing outside of it. After you did what you did, the business wasn't pleasant for me anymore."

"I got a plan," Onyx says. "I'm coming to get you."

Pump, pump, pump, pump…

"What did Gregor do to you after I left?"

Billie smiles and wipes a tear. "Nothing at all, baby."

Onyx shudders. "What's that around your neck?"

"Oh, this? It's a diamond choker."

"Who gave it to you?"

Billie touches the collar, ignores the question. "You know, it made me happy knowing you were free," she says. "I knew you'd come back one day, but while you were out in the world, I was happy for you."

Onyx sighs. "I wasn't happy being without you."

Billie taps her necklace. "Well, tough shit—you best figure out how to be happy without me." She laughs in cruel sounds.

Onyx kneels at her feet. "I'm so sorry, honey."

Billie pushes him away. "As Gregor's messenger, I'm here to deliver his personal invitation to the mansion this evening," she says. "And also a very sincere promise to kill you if you don't come."

Onyx looks into her face. He sees reflections of ancient pain when he gazes into her eyes. Sees bookmarks, empty glasses and pill bottles, mushrooms and rolling papers, vials of unknown liquids, cameras and lights, parties and bands, clean and dirty bed sheets, parades of people splitting her soul into pieces.

Onyx gets to his feet, undresses. "What time?"

Billie whispers, "Six o'clock." Her half-slit eyes gaze at his body. Waves of hormones surge, a lascivious thunder that makes her feline and slinky. She knows his flavors, colors, sizes, smells. Sees only this moment and watches him crawl inside the light bed. Notes the way he pulls the top over him, loves the sound of his voice in that silver tomb. Laughs at how loud the bed is. Stares at the door and waits until he's done cooking.

Billie rises when the tanning bed lights go dark. "Remember how we wanted to be in movies?" she says. "Funny how dreams can turn on you sometimes." Suddenly smiling, she says, "Tonight at six then." She opens the door—*pump, pump, pump, pump.*

"Don't be late," she tells him, closing the door.

Pump, pump, pump, pump

Onyx stares at the goggles in his hand. Stands naked as time passes and passes. Gets dressed and leaves the room too. Wonders how their big dreams failed. Decides not to work out, passes Deskman as he exits, and he waves goodbye.

He runs upstairs. Light-headed and aware, he hops into his car. He finds the highway and a cigarette. Searches his mind, now a pulsing thing filled with ghosts and moving pictures. Swallows his hope. Seeks the path for tonight's descent into the underworld.

He has business with the one who reigns there.

Onyx finds the hotel and begins waiting out the hours.

A quick trip next door to Quick Trip.

He laughs at the jingle-jangle door. Stands at the counter and asks for a long pack of Newports. Ponders a ticket for the lottery and settles for a pile of scratch-offs.

Another pair of jingle-jangles.

Someone looms behind him as he nods to the clerk and leaves the store. Two men follow. The taller one drapes a thick oak tree arm around his shoulders. "Onyx, I can't hurt you without a green light. Besides, you know that karate shit—I want confirmation."

"I killed Shank with that karate shit only because he was too much of a pussy to fight without a knife," Onyx says. "It ain't my fault he was a pussy. Jim's not a pussy—are you a pussy, Benny?"

A shocked chuckle from the tall man. "Go wait in the car, Benny, and don't goddamn hesitate—wait in the fucking car like a good boy."

Benny, pouting piss and vinegar, tucks himself into the sedan. Jim turns his full attention back to Onyx. He squares himself out of his partner's sight line.

"Benny looking at us?"

Onyx speaks through the side of his mouth. "Yeah."

"I hate playing thug, but shitbird wanted a show. Shank's replacement looks like another pussy, doesn't he?"

Onyx nods. "I'm coming back tonight, Jim."

"I know, but that's not why I'm here, son. Look, Gregor's promised to kill Billie if you try to get her out again. I know you, and I know you got a better plan in that head."

Onyx looks away. "I don't have any plan, Jim."

Jim moves closer. "That's bullshit, buddy, because you wouldn't be back if you didn't have one," he says. "Whatever you got worked out won't work out. There's a better way to get rid of Gregor if you can find the strength to be patient. He's almost two-hundred fifty pounds overweight. He won't change his diet or take medication. If you can find a way to be patient, then you can save her."

"Patient for how long? Why won't he just let us go?"

"Doesn't matter, so just be on time tonight, apologize for killing one of his boys, and Gregor will welcome you with open arms. He never liked Shank, but like everyone else, he adores you. Do the right thing and play Prodigal Son, and things'll be fine sooner than you think. You aren't the only one who wants that sonofabitch dead. I'm your friend, young man, so I'm telling you to be patient and trust me. Miracles happen every day."

"Miracles happen? Really?"

Onyx fights his urge to trust the man. And loses. "I'll try, Jim."

Jim squeezes his shoulder. "Good boy," he says. "Now, here comes a fake punch to the gut—quick, no one's watching but Benny-shiffer-brains."

Hitting the ground, Onyx holds his stomach and groans melodramatically. Jim, leaning over, says, "Please, for the love of God, be patient."

And then he's gone.

The rain comes down as Onyx gets up. He watches an ambulance run along the overpass. Picks up his bag and walks to his hotel room. He cleans himself up, checks out, heads back to his car, and makes for Buckhead. West Paces Ferry, Atlanta's curving asphalt River Styx, carries him to the mansion. He stops at the gate.

The guards know his car and name—it's still strange how people simply gravitate towards him—but the pale bony guard refuses to let him to pass without drama.

Gregor's son Cary stands at the driver's window. Relishes the power his father gives him. Thinks he's actually affecting Onyx, who is about to honk the horn and run the gate. Cary squawks into a walkie-talkie.

The bar rises.

Onyx wends around the two-mile driveway with the windows down and breathes scents of moist soil, Georgia pine, and wet dog. Up there in the distance, a mansion beveled deep into the hills squats like a big beige toad. Trees slither along the steep embankment, dropping leaves of every color over the ivy-covered ground.

He parks the car beneath a bone-bare copse of maple and beech. He gets out and trudges down cobblestones, up fieldstone steps along a sidewalk sloping up to a wide stoop and a massive front door. Knocking is like banging on a bank vault or a tomb.

The door opens by remote.

Onyx swallows hard. Heart thumps like a wild thing's. He sees a shadow inside heaving itself up into a massive form—Hamlet's ghost and a second Herod.

Gregor Maxis, the Dixie Porn King, waddles to the trembling guest on the doorstep and embraces him. "Onyx, thou art here, and all that I have is thine," Gregor says, enfolding him with thick haggis arms. "Be glad, for thou art alive again—was lost and now is found." He slurps as he chuckles, the sounds of a fat-man's tar-pasted lungs smacking from years of too many cigars and racks of lamb.

"It's good to see you, Gregor," Onyx says.

The fat man presses avuncular sausage fingers into the shoulders of his prodigal son. "Welcome home, my boy," he says, wheezing and sweating, pulling Onyx by the arm just inside the house. "Can't wait for you to see the new set-up—all the latest equipment."

They laugh as friends.

They pretend to know something the other doesn't.

They prepare for a battle whose time hasn't come.

Suddenly, the fat man stops. "You do this again," Gregor says, thick face dripping with sweat, "I'll make Billie wish she'd died in childbirth. If that doesn't work, I'll make you wish the same thing—understood?"

The words aren't really felt.

Onyx sighs. "What would it take to release Billie from her contract? I'll do anything."

Gregor claps him on the back. "My dear boy, the only thing that would release that minx from my employ is her death or mine."

Sounds of firing weapons inside the mansion interrupt them. The fat man's mouth opens and closes like a grouper, saliva collecting in the corners. His eyes widen. Heard above the new volley of gunshots is Gregor's gasping and curdling blood-filled breathing. Panic and pain and shock propels him forward in utter disbelief.

And Gregor falls like a tree at Onyx's feet.

What the fuck is happening?

Jim's miracle?

His first thought, naturally, was stroke or heart attack (or both)—either way, it's a fucking miracle. Then reality settles in his brain. Never discount the unexpected fury of a woman scorned and battered and abused.

Standing in the fat man's place is Bilouxi, her small hands covered in blood, one of them gripping a dripping steak knife. She yanks the chocker, drops the weapon, and falls into Onyx's arms.

The front door is open.

Sounds of shouting in the long hallway mingle with fighting noises in the driveway.

Jim appears from behind the atrium fountain and takes Billie into his arms. He drapes her like a towel over his shoulder and tells Onyx to follow. Running hunchbacked through the chaos, they weave through the tall shrubs, keeping close to the house as they slip around back.

There's a car idling in the service entrance driveway.

*

There's a smile on Billie's face.

She closes her eyes as the getaway vehicle peels off down the road. Of course, killing Gregor was an easy decision, but she's glad Jim was there to improvise. He saw her raise the knife, so he started the gunfight to cover for it.

She knows she ought to be more appreciative, but she's too busy succumbing to the last bit of her own rescue, thank you very much.

The pills she took are strong.

At first, it was about a little something to take off the edge—she needed a steady hand to kill that greasy fat fuck. Before she knew what was happening, she had an empty bottle in one hand and a knife in the other. Spontaneity was always her favorite plan—why not her own rescue? She sure as hell wasn't going to wait to be pulled from harm's way.

Still, maybe she shouldn't have swallowed the entire bottle. She hears Onyx tell Jim to drive to the nearest hospital. Feels him press his hand to her forehead as he says, "She's taken something—a lot of it."

He slaps her cheeks.

"Billie, baby, open your eyes."

The car speeds ahead faster. Billie blinks, but her rolling eyes weigh the lids. Why should she open them? She's already safe. She's too tired and dreamy to stay awake.

"Sing to me," she whispers. "Sing me to sleep."

"Onyx, keep her awake—two more minutes."

Onyx slaps her cheeks again. "C'mon, baby—stay awake," he says. "You gotta stay awake until we get you to the hospital."

Billie opens her eyes for a moment.

"I'd rather sleep in your lap and dream forever, Onyx—for the first time in years, I feel like I'm in heaven. And I'm so goddamn happy I could die."

*

What the Hurricane Done Brung Us

Excerpt from the novel *Perdido River Bastard*.

Cantonment, Florida—June 10, 1919

Margaret knew should have reached the Wilson place by now. She trudged north along the river with a howling newborn in her arms. His wrist badly broken, the baby screamed himself hoarse between fits of shock and silence.

The early hurricane had begun to assault the watershed, but the storm did not frighten Margaret.

Knowing that Earle Adam Doogan and his men were hunting her down did.

Margaret lost her footing and fell hard on her backside, rattling her teeth and bones. Wobbling to her feet, she searched for landmarks—nothing was familiar.

Swirling in the ravine below were the remnants of a bridge and a mangled carcass of a panther. A wayward branch knocked her down again. "Hell's bells, Lord—I can't do Your work if I breakin' the damn baby," she said, spitting a tooth. "Hep a sinner, Lord!"

As Margaret waited for the vertigo to pass, the ground beneath her collapsed. She tumbled toward the troubled water and rolled into a boulder. Ignoring the pain, she did her best to calm the infant clutched in the crook of her arm.

He's going to die soon, she thought.

The hairs on her arms tingled. A flash of light cracked the air and split the trunk of an oak tree perched on the edge of the wall. The flaming tree fell into the ravine and pinned her, the mud beneath her now like quicksand. Debris collected into dams of dead animals, leaves, wooden posts, toys, and refuse. She needed to free herself.

Spying a row of sapling pines directly above her, Margaret used a sticky trunk to pull herself from the muck. She climbed the charred trunk of the burning tree and passed its curtain of exposed roots at the top of the steep bank. The house she sought was in the clearing ahead—she nearly danced a jig when she saw the windows aglow with light.

Hiking her sopping dress, she went to the house, a beacon shining atop its dark hill, and fell on the steps to the front porch. "Justice Wilson, git out here," Margaret shouted. "You, Justice Wilson!"

A black-haired man holdimng a shotgun and a lantern opened the door. "Margaret Shelby? Is that you, woman? Didn't expect you 'til tomorrow."

"Damnation, Justice—gimme the gun an' take this child," she said.

"Dear Heavenly Father," Justice said. "Who did this to him? Answer me, woman."

"God did it to'm," Margaret spat and went inside the house. "God did it to us when He let Uriah Shelby fill the watershed full of bastards. Tend to the baby while's I tend to my sister—how's Ruth?"

"Baby was stillborn," Justice said. "Ruth doesn't know. Becca took care of her mama when Confederate Jasmine didn't come. She did what you taught her—and I thought she was too young for midwifing."

"Like all men, you're ignorant," Margaret said, tossing her bonnet to the family table as she went to the back room. "See to that baby. Save his life an' you'll have the son Ruth couldn't give you."

"What aren't you telling me, woman?"

There was a long silence. Outside, the wind and rain railed against the house. Inside, Margaret smiled and said, "Behind the bible on the mantle is my flask. Have some whiskey and pack my pipe."

Another squall shook the roof. Justice took the quilt from the rocking chair and placed it on the table. Laying the baby on it, he removed the soiled wrappings and sucked his teeth. A small voice behind him spoke.

"Papa, the storm's loud again."

Tucking raven-colored hair behind her ears, the girl moved beneath his arm and gasped. The baby's white hair, the filth covering his body, the broken bone, and his ripped flesh filled her with pity.

"I thought the baby died, Papa."

Justice calmly set her to task. Becca returned with a basin of soapy water and a wooden spoon from the cupboard. She fetched a quilt and the baby clothes she helped Mama sew, and she watched her father work. He explained what he was doing as he washed the angry flesh, reset the bone, and stitched the skin. The arm was dislocated at the shoulder, but with Papa's help, Becca popped it back in place.

The baby stopped screaming. And when Becca dressed him and cradled him in her arms, the baby stopped shaking. "Such blue eyes," she cooed. "Will Mama feed him? I can make a pap if I need to."

Justice had not thought about feeding the child until now. He said a silent prayer to God asking His forgiveness for not grieving for his dead son. There was new life in need of saving still. Becca was as bright as a polished silver pot and knew not tell her mother about the child she held.

"Hello, little brother," she said.

Justice looked up when Margaret touched his arm. "She's weak as a kitten, but strong enough to feed him. Becca-girl, take him in. Say nothing 'bout him, that's a lamb." Margaret took the bloody sheets she had been hiding behind her to the sink. "I told Ruth his arm got twisted up in the cord and broken when she pushed him out. No, you sit while I do my business in here. I'll tell you everything when Confederate Jasmine comes. Just know he's yours."

With the body of his stillborn son cleaned and wrapped for burial, Justice went to see his wife. The copper-metal scent of blood greeted them before the light of the candles did. Ruth smiled, her cheeks pale pink as the infant suckled hungrily at her breast.

Justice sat beside her. "Does it hurt?"

Ruth winced. "More'n the labor—I had a dream he was dead, but he can't be. Look at the white hair on his head. Is the storm here yet?"

Justice shook his head. "The worst is hours off, so don't worry yourself." He helped Ruth button her gown and took the baby. "What's he called?"

"Ewell Curtis Wilson," she said with a smile. "A strong baby needs a name to help him survive this God-forsaken watershed." She yawned and said, "Ewell Curtis, his head looks like a cotton bud."

Later, as the hurricane crept up the river, Becca read

from the Book of Matthew in her room. Justice held his living son at the table, as Margaret smoked her corncob pipe and sipped corn whiskey from her flask. The scratches on her face and neck looked as if the devil had whipped her.

"Ruth's right," Margaret said. "God has a plan for him, which goes double for us sinners takin' care of him. He's a cursed blessin', if you ask me."

"Margaret Shelby, I won't have curse talk in my house," he said, his eyes narrowed. "I don't care what you or your sisters say about the taint of Uriah Shelby's blood. I'll put you out like a cat."

"You'll taste my knuckles if you try," she said, trying not to smile. "These folk will see this albino baby as cursed whether you will or won't, so git right with the talk. Pray for strength to hep the boy weather the storm his life will be. After God's done with him, he'll suffer more than the Devil's own. It's always God's children who suffer most."

"Woman, what are you not telling me?"

Margaret took a drink. "He's the bastard son of JJ Doogan," she said. "Confederate Jasmine's youngest daughter Echo gave birth last night—she died. My sisters would drown Doogan spawn for sport, but he's the grandson of Confederate Jasmine too, so... I set out this morning to get here before the storm hit, but I had to hide in Cantonment."

"Who's after this boy, Margaret?"

The sound of Becca's shuffling ended the conversation. "Papa, do you know those men in the backyard," she asked. "Their swearing woke me."

Margaret gripped her arms. "They see you?"

"No'm, my candle was out," she said. "They talked about a nigger baby the Shelby witch brought here. Aunt Margaret, you didn't bring a nigger baby here. That's baby's white as Christmas snow."

Justice gently patted her. "Don't say nigger, Becca," he said, grabbing the shotgun. "Margaret, who are they?"

"Earle Adam Doogan and some of his kin," she replied. "I hoped this storm would stop 'em in Cantonment, but I knew it was a small chance. I'll pay for it. My life ain't worth that much."

Justice swallowed. "Becca take the baby in to Mama, lock the door and say nothing."

"Yes, Papa."

Justice turned to Margaret. "Get the gun on the shelf over the cupboard—protect my family, and that includes you, you old harpy. Earle Doogan isn't so powerful without his entire posse. He'll leave soon, one way or another."

"But you got HIS property," Margaret countered, pointing to the bedroom. "The property that'll be suckling at Ruth's teat while you're squaring off with his evil grandpa."

Justice glanced at the neatly folded lump of clean sheets at the end of the table. He was surprised at how quickly the thought came, that his dead son might be their salvation. "Margaret, you're mistaken," he said. "There's nothing in this house, alive or dead, belonging to Earle Adam Doogan."

Outside, the wind brought in the rain sideways. His eyes adjusted to the darkness as he searched for trespassers. Justice heard no one, saw no one, but he felt eyes watching him. He knew the river and its tributaries intimately. He had a sixth sense about life here. A strange quiet from the west told him eyes were on him.

A gust from the back of the house carried the stench of sour sweat, chewing tobacco, moonshine, and blood. It was the perfect place for hiding—Justice could see the spot from the end of the porch. He aimed his shotgun high at the trees there and squeezed the trigger, the blast bringing down a loose branch from a tall elm.

"That's your warning," he shouted, lowering the barrel. "Earle Doogan, go and live, or stay and die." Wind was his answer. Aiming, he squeezed the trigger and fired.

"JUSTICE WILSON, I GOT THE NIGGER JAS-MINE WOMAN," shouted a voice.

Justice lowered his gun. "Jasmine?"

No reply came, only the dim light of a newly lit kerosene lamp peeking through the trees. Two men, the one holding the lamp and the other dragging a large sack, headed across the lawn for the porch. The one with the light was limping badly—the one with the sack struggled against gusts of wind and the prisoner inside his bag.

Justice aimed. "Earle Adam Doogan, I'm a God-fearing man, but you're trespassing, and I protect what's mine."

"I protect what's mine—all's I want is justice, Justice," Earle spat, thumbing behind him. "I got an ace shot in them trees and his pistol's pointed at yer face. Them Shelby bitches kilt my JJ. I know Margaret stole my bastard grandson. I'll trade what I got in my sack for my property you got in your house. Be still, you nigger piece-of-shit!" Earle kicked the soiled canvas bag.

Justice winced. Earle's nephew Lucas lurched, nearly dropping the lantern. "I need to sit," he said, dry heaving. "I'm cold, Uncle Earle."

"Quit whinin'," Earle snapped. "We'll git the hell gone soon's I got what's mine. Boy, don't you bleed out. Justice Wilson, give me my half-nigger grandson. Dead, alive, don't matter. I ain't protecting life. I'm protecting my family honor and my own goddamn legacy. My name will be remembered with fear and awe for generations."

The front door opened. Margaret Shelby walked onto the porch with her shotgun aimed at the man. "Earle Doogan, you ain't fit to lick the devil's feet," she said. "I'm a better shot than anybody you got hidin' in them trees. Leave the bag an' get the hell gone, or I'll kill two Doogans just to give a pair of angels upstairs some wings."

"Goddammit, y'all killed my boy!"

"He wasn't no boy—he was a monster named JJ Doogan. It didn't matter to him that he had two little ones at home. He had to plant his evil seed inside an innocent girl. So, we cut him to bloody bits for a secret backyard burial. You won't find no grave. Earle Adam, since I ha'n't slept in two days, my trigger finger's itchy as a chigger bug bite."

Earle pulled his prisoner out by the nape of her neck. Confederate Jasmine was an older woman, but her eyes were wide and defiant, and they blazed with fire. A knife suddenly in his hand, Earle pressed the blade to her face. "I wonder if I got me a bleeder," he said, caressing her skin. He removed the gag but then drove the tip of his blade into her shoulder.

"Don't cut her!" Margaret shouted.

Earle Adam whistled a strange bird call to the trees—there was no response. "I told my boy there to hold off—I'll kill this nigger and die a glorious death, if Margaret shoots proper. Either way, I protect what's mine," he said. "Justice, control that Shelby bitch or get another dog."

Margaret spat. "A Doogan couldn't bluff hisself out of a fist fight with a dumb crippled blind girl."

Justice raised a hand. "Margaret, JJ's dead bastard isn't

worth more than Confederate Jasmine's life." He turned to give Margaret a hard stare until she lowered her gun. "Get the bundle for Earle."

Margaret understood what needed doing and went inside the house. Justice Wilson knew this was their chance. He fought back tears when that evil man took his stillborn son. After Margaret helped Confederate Jasmine from the sack, Earle threw in the lifeless lump given to him.

Suddenly, Lucas Doogan dropped his lantern, keeling over face-first in the mud, dead as a stump. The wick burned brightly, revealing a dark red pool around the steps, and went out.

Earle kicked the body. "Now I gotta haul yer ass home," he said, glaring at Justice as he stuffed his dead nephew in the canvas sack. Tying it shut, he hoisted it on his shoulder and smiled. As the wind blustered, and the clouds emptied their water, he calmly stood in the middle of it. He looked at each face before him, and then, as if he'd been a neighbor stopping by, he tipped an imaginary hat. "Y'all have a pleasant evenin'." Then Earle Adam Doogan headed for the line of trees and vanished into the night.

"That man murdered your son and husband, Jasmine," Justice said. "His son murdered your son-in-law, raped your daughter, and kidnapped you just to get his hands on his dead son's bastard. This isn't over."

"Things ain't what they seem," Confederate Jasmine said, wincing.

"Jazzy, you're bleedin' like a stuck pig," Margaret said, helping. "Shoulder needs cleanin' an' sewin'—I doubt Earle Adam washes his knife."

"I'm fine—I just drank too much hurricane's all," Confederate Jasmine said. "You can play seamstress while I drink me some corn and tell this saint what we've set in motion."

"If he's a saint, then I'm the Virgin Mary," Margaret said with a hearty laugh.

"He's saint enough. And he deserves the truth." Confederate Jasmine touched his cheek and added, "Steel yourself, Justice. We had to cover tracks to do what we did tonight. They won't stay hidden forever."

Margaret spat. "Well, at least we got a barn out of it."

Confederate Jasmine laughed. "Biggest tombstone in the South. And the perfect place to hide a set of twins separated at birth."

"What have you two done?"

Neither woman answered. They went into the house and left Justice Wilson alone on the porch.

*

Streetwise Astrolabe

Originally published by *Cerulean Rain*.

Raymond Chandler said anything could happen when the Santa Anas started blowing. That might sound like hyperbole where you live, but not in a place where fantasy and metaphor are often literal truths.

Autumn was cruel last year. Dry desert air came off the Sierra Nevada and blew us to Kingdom Come. Those winds were anything but magical. They fueled wildfires that raged unlike anything in recent memory. A cinematic hell from the mountains to the coast, thousands of acres ablaze as California sinners burned on live television.

There's nothing like watching perfect people in peril, but even great TV is an illusion. Because I was in the business, I was part of the same machine that spun tragedy into box-office gold. There's an art to making ugly reality into a national commodity, and I'd sold my soul to do it.

The death of your child will do that to you.

The eighteenth of October would have been his twenty-second birthday. My wife and I had a condo near Hollywood Boulevard. I needed time to get my head together before the anniversary, so I stayed there to read scripts I'd been putting off. Maggie kept a solitary vigil at our home outside the city in case the fires spread. The night before Josh's birthday, the fires moved into Los Angeles, and I was in the middle of it.

It wasn't the burning of Atlanta, but it was real enough to scare the shit out of me and take me to the brink of something dark.

I'd hoped my time alone would ease tomorrow's pain. The fire made hope an illusion, and one you can't spin into anything. My boy was gone, and I'd made plans long ago for my own 'big sleep' if ever I came undone, and it seemed that I had. But the winds shifted, and strange things were lurking inside them.

I can't say exactly what things—it's been almost a year and I still don't effing know what happened. All I can say is that something I can't explain saved my life.

I remember standing on my front porch as the ash fell like snow and thick, puce-colored clouds began to roll over the city. I said a little desperate prayer, and in a singular bi-polar moment, an urge to end it all became an urge to take a midnight stroll.

It wasn't a George Bailey moment, but it was sudden.

I was jonesing for some Chinese takeout and a long walk down Hollywood Boulevard in the middle of that smoke-filled night. A secret death wish, perhaps, but I didn't care.

A shitload of anything goes was waiting. Santa Anas were pulling, demanding that I join a night that somehow belonged only to me.

By sunrise, I'd learn that Chandler was right about those goddamn winds.

*

It's two in the morning. The air is heavy. Smoke roils in mucous-yellow fog that makes the street seem more back-lot than thoroughfare. Honking cars filled with young men raising hell, wandering homeless pushing grocery carts like hoards of shopping zombies, and flailing sirens of fire trucks and police cruisers. You can almost sense the old road beneath it, one splitting rows of seedy bars and tattoo parlors, flashing marquees above adult bookstores and XXX theaters. A road Starsky and Hutch might have trolled after a hot Huggy Bear tip.

Over there, a girl emerges from one shadow and becomes another. There, a young man with buggy eyes floats above the sidewalk. And there, an old drag queen in fishnets and make-up hobbles away on broken heels. Young and old, they're flesh and blood ghosts.

I'm one of them now.

I'm on a bench looking at my son's school picture, Josh forever smiling like he'd swallowed joy in whole chunks. I marvel at how much of Maggie is there—the nose, the deep green eyes, the skin coloring. Even places inside harbor his mother's pieces—her love of details and small things, her need to devour books, her proclivity for solitude, her infectious laughter. Now there was a boy who laughed since the day he was born.

The winds shift into warmer gusts.

One minute, I'm alone with my misery, trying not to choke on it, and the next minute, I'm not alone. A teenage girl comes out of nowhere—boom, she's standing a short distance from my bench. She doesn't notice me as I study her. At first glance, she's just another urchin hooker. She's almost pretty, too-thin and too-young, but her skin glows like amber in the lamplight, and when the wind lifts her hair, she becomes stunning. When she sees that I'm staring, she spins around for me.

"Central casting?" I ask her.

She laughs. "Baby, I know this street looks like a set, but it ain't. Now, some folks used to call me the Midnight Angel like I was somebody. I got me a Charlie's Angels wig, my bangles and my prints, my stockings for my two long dark-n-lovelies. See? A little bubblin' brown sugar, clean as snow, disease-free. Don't worry, baby, I ain't gonna work you, but behold the only woman who can make a constellation out of names on a sidewalk."

"Midnight Angel suits you."

"I know, baby," she tells me. She bends strategically at the curb and begins what she calls her black magic. A subtle stocking adjustment becomes a peepshow for passing cars, the lighting of a cigarette is acrobatic foreplay, and a saunter makes this slip of a thing a courtesan.

It's impressive, and as a man, all you can do is wonder what the minx is like in bed.

A force of nature demands respect, prostitute or not, but I can tell this girl kills wolves as she dances a choreography that makes you want her. It is a purity that borders on innocence.

I think of William Blake.

Little Lamb, who made thee?

Midnight Angel hurls a stone at a screeching car, peeling away as its howling occupants dangle male parts through its opened windows.

"Motherfuckers!" she screams.

So much for Blake.

Midnight stands under the lamp for a moment slowly

walks into a thick patch of whirling haze. As I size her up, she moves to the bench, sits, and smiles. With that one dimple in her left cheek and the tiny freckles on her nose, she's suddenly twelve years-old, covered in Mama's make-up and evening clothes, looking at her reflection in a mirror behind the closet door.

"See how the winds roll this smoke?" she says. "At this time of night, it's like movie fog—it ain't real. Whenever the two o'clock hour comes, crazy doings like the Santa Anas start fucking things up in here. Always makes a mess for folks, living or dead. Baby, are you done with that sweet-and-sour chicken, because I'm starving."

I hand her the half-eaten box of food.

"You're just a kid," I tell her as she finishes it.

Midnight gets to her feet. "I'm a wise old ho, baby."

She adjusts her purse strap, and twirls a sexy little dervish between a pair of Latino thugs and settles inside a meandering group of frat boys. She weaves spells with smiles until one of them pats her backside. Before he can duck, she swings her purse. He screams under his arms, muttering phrases like 'just looking' and 'I'll be your daddy' while crab-walking away from her. She hits him with that brick-heavy clutch again and again, popping him with it on every other word. He bolts to his friends who scatter into the smoke. Midnight bows when I applaud.

I begin to understand that this must be a game played and won every time she's out here. When a vet in tattered fatigues drops his bag-wrapped ripple bottle, she is there to steady him before he falls. The vet thanks her and asks a question I can't hear. By her face, I know what he's asked.

Midnight shakes her head. She touches his arm and flashes a smile. Compassionate, yes, but she's also including him in her game. With a dramatic flourish, she shouts, "No, baby. I appreciate your service, but I ain't a troop ship. You ain't gonna be marching home on me, Johnny. Go on down to Bob Hope's star. Maybe the USO can help. Or Cheryl, yeah. She looks like one of them ABBA bitches. Give her some money, money, money, Fernando. Take a chance on her. She'll be your dancing queen."

The vet laughs so hard he drops his bottle. He kicks it along the sidewalk as he disappears into the smoke.

Midnight returns to the bench and lights a cigarette.

The winds blow through half-filled streets. A dog barks a question from the west. An answer comes from the east. Smoke and falling ash diffuses the light into white silence— no sounds of violence, no pleas for help, no alarms, no distant music, no screams, no bottles.

I'm looking at Josh's school picture again.

"Who's that, baby?" asks Midnight, pointing.

"It's my son—tomorrow's his birthday."

She reaches for it. "Lemme see. Oh my, what a handsome boy."

"He was the best, most perfect thing I've ever done— each October gets worse and worse."

Midnight tosses her cigarette. "I'm sorry, baby—who took him?"

"How did you know someone killed him?"

She shrugs. "Just a guess."

"The morning he turned seventeen, he played hooky from school and went to the park with some friends," I tell her. "In broad daylight, a man walked up to him and stabbed him in throat." I show her where. "That was five years ago."

"The police ever catch him?"

"No, they haven't—I mean, they tell me they did, but I don't believe it," I say. "My wife thinks I'm losing my mind. She says I'm going to lose her if I keep working the way I do. If I don't let him go."

Midnight returns the photo. "Baby, you can stare all you want at that smiling boy's face, but it won't bring him back. It won't heal your heart. It won't help you let him go."

"I know."

"Then why do you drown in a dead boy's smile?" she asks. "That's right, I said it. Your boy's dead. You know better than to cleave to nothing, but you keep holding on. It's made you blind to your woman, and you keep holding on. You better change before she leaves your wallowin' ass."

"Maggie has his face," I shout. My voice echoes. "I'm sorry."

Midnight laughs. "Get mad all you want. You know I'm right. Your woman's who you need to be holding, baby. Your boy's dead. She's alive. Tomorrow's coming whether you want it to or not, whether you're alive or not. All you can do is bend to the inevitable."

My face burns now.

I say nothing as I watch the wildfires glow bright over the hills and the distant horizon. I'm wondering why I'm still out on these ash-stained streets. I keep telling myself that I'm brain-dumping a week of story treatments and screenplays, old black and white movies, and bad dreams. It's hard to tell what's real in all this rolling smog.

Midnight takes my hand. "A young woman named Yolanda Washington used to walk these stars back in the day," she says. "She had a hard life, but was smart enough to get herself together before it was too late. She got her GED and took college night classes. She stopped hooking every day. She went for walks, played chess in the park with the old men, and collected books folks threw into the garbage. She had trouble letting go of these stars though. In the end, she was too late to save herself."

"What happened?"

"The Hillside Strangler dumped her at Forest Lawn."

"I remember the Hillside Strangler," I say. "Thirty years ago—you can't be old enough to remember that."

"I was spinning your pathetic white ass a story with

a lesson," Midnight says with a laugh. "Better figure out what Yolanda's story can teach you before the sun comes up. Every soul has to learn three things about living in the world—what to keep, what to let go, and what to remember. Decide those things tonight, baby, and you'll wake up to a different day."

Midnight lets go of my hand. I can't speak. Her up-turned palm on my mouth holds great power.

I can only wonder at what she's smiling about.

Greater gusts swirl dust, pebbles, and grit until little devils become funnels that coalesce into a mass of spinning smoke and haze. A hole opens in the thick, low sky wide enough to see the stars hanging in a night that's moving from black to blaze. Somewhere, I think, a planet explodes.

I get to my feet. "Who are you?"

Midnight rises too. "Next time you pray for someone to watch over you, baby, you better be more specific."

"But how—" I begin.

But the rest spills onto the ground as I watch her slink down her stretch of the Walk of Fame. *How did she know?*

Midnight Angel, a streetwise astrolabe who measures

the distance between her stars as she navigates this boulevard of sin. She moves into the rolling smoke and shadows, and then she's gone.

It's about as Hollywood an exit you get.

What remains unsaid, what lingers, isn't the uncertainty of an unexplained event, but the certainty of an unspoken promise.

So, I'm sitting on a bench at two thirty in the morning. The air is lighter. I'm alone. I drop the picture of my dead son, and a wind sweeps it into the hazy night. As I watch it disappear, I think of Maggie and weep.

*

I was dreaming of winds when poking woke me.

Opening my eyes, I saw the gnarled stick that did it and then the face of the man who held its end. A brown-toothed grin, tattered fatigues—it was the man who dropped his ripple bottle last night.

Last night happened, didn't it?

"Jesus, my heart hurts."

"Better get 'fore the police come," he said. "They patrol this area 'round 'bout now. They like bench warmers as much as hookers."

Last night's orgy of haze and smoke had nearly dissipated. The pre-dawn sky was awash in early gloaming hues of purple and peach. Ghosts were sleeping, living souls were rising, and my mind was unfolding with too many questions. Looking at the vet, I nodded to the space beside me and checked my watch—its hands were locked at 2:32.

I replayed the night. I'd left the condo at midnight, walked an hour or so, grabbed some food and sat down for a bit, and then talked with a prostitute. I shook my head, aching from a night of smoke inhalation, but when did I pass out? The taste in my mouth said days.

Had I finally succumbed to one of my own plot devices?

The old homeless vet began snoring. I took a couple fives and twenties from my wallet and stuffed them inside his shirt pocket. I smiled when I didn't wake him. Morning let out a little more light on my return to the condo.

Turning from a narrow side street, I walked toward my building's unsightly backyard, a nuclear winter landscape after last night.

There was a pathetic warble in a bare almond tree, and it seemed that happy birds were not in California.

I swear this poor thing was singing the blues.

Heading around to the front yard, I went to my unit on the first floor, the only one with a private entrance and porch. When I got to the stoop, I froze. Maggie was there, her head propped against a post as her body lay draped over the softer parts of our canvas luggage. She must have forgotten a key, yes, but why did she come? When? Had the wildfires spread? Was our house in danger?

My heart pounded as I climbed the steps and sat down, and I must have gazed at her for ten or fifteen minutes before I moved. Finally, I brushed away strands of her hair. "Good morning."

Her green eyes fluttered open, and when she saw me, she burst into tears, throwing her arms around me until those first sobs ebbed. Kissing came next, but then the tears started up again, muffling her words. Shushing apologies in her ear, I told her about falling asleep on a bench, that the smoke had dehydrated me and made me pass out.

"You look like shit," she said.

"You should smell my breath."

She laughed. "I think I'll pass."

Maggie began grooming me like a monkey. She wiped ashes from my shirt and pulled a half-stuck blob of chewing gum off my sleeve. A leaf had burrowed into my hair and a ladybug behind my ear. She brushed a white smear from my blue jeans and began to cry again. I held her. Strong as she was, my wife was all about the water works—seriously, she was one of those TV commercial weepers.

It meant keeping tissues handy. She pulled a box from the duffle bag under her backside. She blew her nose and wiped her eyes, and as per usual, the used ones piled up in my hand.

"I had a bad dream," Maggie said, blowing into a new tissue, "but when I called, you didn't answer. I know I said you were better off without me right now. But I had to know if you were alive. And yes, that's an overnight bag, but it doesn't mean I want to stay because it was for just in case you asked me. So if you want to ask me to go or stay, then I'd be okay with—"

"I want you to stay," I said.

Holding my face to check reality, she asked, "You do? I can stay?"

I was about to say yes, but the weeping started again, this time with added birdsong from the backyard—it was a bizarre mix of depressed minimalist warbling and Maggie's sniffling.

"So, you're okay?" she asked "You didn't get raped?"

"No," I said. "You wanna tell me about your dream?"

"Josh came to me," she said. "He wanted me to help him find you because you didn't know where home was anymore. Why do I only dream in clichés? Anyway, he was taking me to you and then I was falling through a sky full of stars. I woke before hitting ground."

Cold chills bloomed on my arms. "Sky full of stars?"

Maggie nodded and looked at her own gooseflesh too, and all the while, that goddamn melancholy bird in the backyard warbled its avian dirge.

"I'm having déjà vu," she said.

Me too, Maggie.

"What time did you get here, honey?" I asked.

"The dream woke me at two-thirty two on the nose," she

told me. "I got up to call you and then drove down here."

Showing her my watch, I said, "Maggie, look at the time. Look."

She didn't know what to say.

Hell, I didn't know if I could believe it either. Fear of synchronicity eased when, for a lightning moment, I couldn't remember why we were sitting there. I couldn't remember the winds or the fires, my walk down the boulevard, the vet I'd given all my cash to, or Midnight Angel.

There was only my son standing in the middle of all that nothingness, waving goodbye.

I had visions of the electricity of his seventeen years—Josh blowing out two candles on his cake, a broken leg cast covered in scripts of inky spaghetti, his mud-covered baseball uniforms, his mismatched junior prom tuxedo, his rusty Camaro beater that he'd bought with his own money—and then he was gone.

"What is it, honey?" Maggie asked.

I took a deep breath and smiled. "I just love you, wife."

She took my hand as the sweetest kiss of cool air brushed us. No hint of burning things or what had fallen during the night. Only the scents of clean pine and moist soil and watered grasses remained. And they hovered like whispers until we left the front porch.

I don't know exactly when we moved inside.

I don't know why we didn't talk about our shared odd coincidence, why I didn't tell her about the rest of my strange night, or why I felt that keeping it unexplained was best.

I don't know when our clothes came off, when we fell into bed, or exactly how many times we made love (I say four—she says three). And I don't know when we got dressed for dinner or what time we returned.

What I do know is that there were twenty-two candles on the birthday cake we'd brought home from the restaurant. I know Maggie opened all the windows in the apartment when cooler breezes blew in from the west.

I know that when we fell back into bed, either before the news or after the wine, we made love four times (she says two). And I know eight months and twenty days later, my bride had a little girl—seven pounds and two ounces and her daddy's blue eyes.

I know someone was watching over us the night we

made her. I know because we both slept in kinder dreams ever afterward. Dreams of a lost son found, an ember of love rekindled and renewed.

And always, a midnight sky filled with soft stars—

—and warm winds.

*

D. B. Patterson

Midnight's Rhapsody

Character monologue from *The Gray Man*—

inspiration for the previous story.

(YOLANDA WASHINGTON enters. She
storms DC, like a hurricane.)

ATTENTION, MOTHERFUCKERS! THE MID-
NIGHT ANGEL IS CLOSE AT HAND. BEHOLD MY
GLORY, ALL YOU HEATHEN BITCHBABIES! Shut-
up, Cheryl! Damn, girl—you need therapy. And you best
get away from my walk, honey. I'll bitch-slap your ass back
to Sweden or Iceland or wherever it is you white bitches

think you hail from.

(Pause before she speaks to audience.)

Every night and every day I walk this boulevard of fame. These stars to those—twilight to moonlight—and half the time they're both one and the same—seems like I never see the sun. Piss me off, sometimes—my feet hurt. Back aches. But it pays, baby. It pays. My friend Daisy's all foxy now. She got herself a blonde Dolly Parton wig to hide her perpetually nappy head—men wouldn't touch her otherwise. Scary bitch out of make-up.

(She 'plays' both parts.)

"Do I look like a Daisy or a Jolene?" "Is this a trick question?" I said: "You look like a bumpkin bitch-baby." I called her Bitch-Baby—she called me the Vampire Princess. 'Cause she'd say I looked like one of them Blackula Bitches. I didn't have no goddamn 'fro. I looked more like a Brown Farah Fuckin' Faucet Majors. And I should have had my own star on the walk. Cuz I sho nuff did it every damn night. Walking on these legs. Oh, honey damn legs, yes, sweet Lord. Legs. Look at 'em—see 'em up to my neck. Wanna good rub down up the town and back-a-make you feel good? White brown make you holler—twenty dollars? Mmm-mmm, no baby, no. I ain't. Cheap. I know, I know, but I'm too damn fine—a little bubblin' brown sugar, clean & disease & drug & stain free.

(To offstage person.)

Shut-up! I'll kick your ass you lay a hand on my—

(To another offstage person.)

Motherfucker! Oh, hey, Baby—what you need? Good time? What you want? Fast time? Got the time? Your place, mine?

(Again, speaking to more offstage persons.)

Oh, no you didn't! You can look, you can ALWAYS look at Yolanda Washington, but you can never touch unless I say so. I ain't got no pimp. I am my OWN pimp. And no, you ain't my Daddy neither. I know this because: a) you are not chocolate love; b) you are not chocolate love; and c) I ain't fucked you, and my daddy used to fuck me until I left home when I was eleven. And no amount—uh-uh—no, take it, I don't care how much it is. Daddy? Motherfucker. No amount is gonna make me thank you hard enough, blow enough, fuck enough for me to make ME your baby-bitch woman, sniveling and crawling, rolling 'round for you. I am Yolanda Washington. YOU HEAR ME?! Motherfucker. Cross my goddamn Delaware. Fuck me? Go fuck yourself, little white dick child. Paint my picture while you're at it. I am your black female president. Just walk away, motherfucker.

(Turning.)

Now what? Oh. I'm sorry, baby. Yeah, here's some smooth talking—

(To audience.)

'Scuse me, folks.

(Back to 'customer'.)

Respect the woman you fuck. YOU must know that you are in the presence of the Almighty Wonder Woman of Oz—that's $150, and you'd better believe me, baby, I am worth every little and big bill of a Yolandollar Washington, Lincoln, Jackson, Grant, or Franklin you pay—boy, don't insult me. My pussy will turn you into Jesus. And you will never want to be with another woman after I've had my way with you. On your knees and sing praise. You got me, the Sistah Goddess, to show you how, just how, God made man and woman to be. Alright boy—be gone—I ain't got time to explain your own ignorance to you. Just take your $30 dollar cunt coupons down to the discount disease-ridden lice-crab-crawling unclean skanky ho bungalow down a block or two. Get your rocks off—then save up—cause you'll be back. When you do come back, do it Monday or Wednesday. I got night classes on Tuesdays and Thursdays.

(Attention back to audience.)

Folks be acting up tonight. Yeah, I been walking the walk so many times, can't count—I can't count. Drive by, stop by, shoot 'em up—shoot 'em in. Up in me. On me—over my black rainbow. Every night. This is my turf. This boulevard of broken poonanie. But, my home? See that door? That's where I sleep—and dream. I live there. I never

ever sleep where I fuck. And no phone. You want Yolanda? You come out here—standing on this spot is my phone, and I can see who wants me when they stand here. I just suddenly appear—the Midnight Angel. Yolanda Washington. Meet 'em here—see 'em from there—but I fuck 'em over there. It's clean and I know the boy-child manager. Shame about that boy, saying he loves me like a fool—well, he THINKS he loves me like he says. Boys sometimes say it when they want to save a woman in trouble. I'll save my own damn self. I take night classes. I have a student ID. And damn it, I'm busy with other things besides fucking.

(Addresses 'customer' offstage.)

I see you in my—periphery, baby. I said I'm—oh.

(Turning toward the 'customer'.)

Busy. Hmm. Damn—hey. Hey. Why are YOU looking for a ho? What's the wrong with you? Dick too small? No? And muscles—what's wrong with the bitches in your world? What, baby? It's your birthday. Oh. Damn, you're cute, but I am busy. Damn. I tell you what—you come back in an hour, honey. OK? I mean that. One hour. And I'll give you a discount. Too. OK? Now lemme see—turn around for Yolanda—damn, look at his ass. Hey! You bring your fine ass back in an hour, and I'll take the night off and give you a freebie. It's my birthday, too. Yeah. Bitches have birthdays. And you're my present—

(Turning to another.)

And I wouldn't fuck YOU, you old cracker, if you paid me in gold Spanish doubloons. Hey, don't be hatin' me for having standards and telling the motherfucking gospel truth. Best read my tome, asshole. The Gospel of Yolanda was too goddamn good for the Bible!

(Pause.)

Where was I? Oh—right. Daisy. Daisy bitch-baby. Damn her calves. Daisy Goddamn Dolly-Fuck-a-Ho. Couldn't be by herself. Work by herself. Fuck by herself. Got herself in big trouble. Daisy wanted a pimp, but I said to her, "NO, DaisyBaby. Those men are evil. They will own you." And she's all like, "But, Midnight, please. Just come with me. I need you."

(Pause.)

So, we get there, this place in the way fool far a-god-damn-way, so she can meet him. I'm thinking we gotta go. This ain't right. This man looks at Daisy and says, "You got the list?" I turn to my girl and say, "What list?" She pulls out this little book from her purse and says, "My list of clients, Midnight." Clients? I HAD CLIENTS. Daisy had stragglers and jive-turkeys—don't get me started. Daisy made a FAKE list of regulars. Did she tell ME? Oh, hell, no. If I knew she was meeting a new pimp with a list of lies, then I woulda beat her ass with it. Pimps gotta have a reason to bring bitches on board. Fine, I understand that. But a fake list? And me WITH her and that fake list? Yeah, I woulda put her stupid ass in a hospital. SAFE and ALIVE in a hospital. Daisy didn't know that list was gonna get us both killed.

(Pause.)

She didn't know her pimp-to-be was the Hillside Strangler. Talk about bad motherfuckingluck. That man wasn't stupid. He called the numbers. When they didn't check out, he and his business partner took us both out. Right there on the fucking spot.

(Turning toward an offstage person again.)

I know my ass is fine, oh—you geriatric no-tooth limp-dick motherfucker—I'm busy talking to folks—I got half a mind to—

(To audience.)

'Scuse me.

(Back to offstage rude man.)

Motherfucker. Yeah, and I got needs too. I needs to put my feet up your asshole—pop your spleen out that nasty crusty face of yours—I don't care if you fought in the war—I appreciate your service—but I am not a troop ship—and I don't fuck stinky drunks with bad teeth—No, baby. No. Johnny, you ain't gonna be marchin' home on Yolanda—so best you move yourself down to Bob Hope's star—maybe the USO can help you out.

(After a pause, she calls out.)

Maybe it's that white bitch Cheryl Inga Svengahasen you want—yeah, she's one of—hey, motherfucker, not too close. If you'll shut up, I'm trying to tell your high ass that she's that blonde bitch from ABBA. Yeah—she is. Go on down there—that's the Name of the Game. I swear. Just holler out an SOS, scream Voulez Vous, and throw her some Money, Money, Money. Take a Chance on her, Fernando. She'll be your Dancing Queen.

(Pause. To audience.)

I didn't want to die.

(Pause.)

But you people, I bet you didn't know Yolanda Washington before now, did you? The Hillside Strangler? Yeah, you knew about him. But me? Not so much. Well, I died October 17, 1977. I died because I was in the wrong place at the wrong time. Because I wanted to help a friend.

(Pause.)

Motherfuckers.

(Pause.)

And then, like I was a newborn baby still-birthed into a world beyond, the police found me. And what do you think the world got from that? A naked, black prostitute wrapped in a bag, dumped on the side of the road. A dead, ashy nigger ho is what the world saw. Not newsworthy. I wasn't worthy of being any other kind of news.

(Pause.)

I was making my own way, you know. Doing the best I could with the cards I was dealt. I saw my worth. I knew my worth. After I got my GED, I got into community college. I would've left this boulevard in less than a year. Goddammit, I WAS newsworthy! My life may not have been yours, but I didn't have options when I came out here. I had to MAKE my options appear. Goddammit, I WAS newsworthy! I would've been on Oprah one day because I made my life different from the one given to me. Me, Yolanda Washington. I was newsworthy.

(Pause.)

So, fuck all you people. I watched Bruce Lee movies at that little theatre down the street. I ate Chinese food after my classes. I read old poetry books that people threw in the garbage. I played chess with the old men in the park by my church—and I let this Mexican boy walk me home sometimes. Here, to my Sidewalk of Stars. I talked to him after class. I—I liked that boy. I did. I liked him so much that I let him hold my hand. And he would smile at me with those bright teeth and big brown eyes.

(Pause.)

A week before they found me, he walked me to my star. Then I walked to my home, to my front door just there. And then I let him kiss me goodnight. And it was like I'd never been kissed before that. My God. Anyway, I never saw him again. That's fine because I'm free now. I'm up there in the evening sky with all the ladies of the night who were killed and left naked for the world to see and then NOT see. And I'm here to say to you that WE MATTERED.

(Pause. Holds back tears.)

Count us ALL—you'll run out of numbers. Our lights burn the night from black to blaze, so be amazed when you look up to see the moon. God put us all up there to watch down on you. I'm that sparkling one. See, when I died, God lifted me into the bright midnight, where the stars are made of spirit and fire, and made me immortal. God made me the Constellation Yolanda. That's the gospel truth.

(Pause.)

So, Amen, Motherfuckers. Amen.

(Yolanda exits. Blackout.)

*

Color of Echoes

Originally published by *Ramble Underground*.

Morning.

Half-naked.

Night-beaten.

Drug-drenched.

Two lovers sit, fatally facing each other. Woman, magnetized and full-frontal. Man, half-cocked and quiet. They smoke and talk. He is leaving today.

She stands and paces. Ignores his gaze, so cold and full of blame. She looks over a shoulder and pleads with the sun to turn around for another day. She blows cigarette smoke.

Swallows bittersweet and sour sips from her half-glass of something watered down after all-night bumps. Three days of wear and tear in a descending tunnel of winds.

Light is evil, she thinks—*and why?*

Because it paints the morning Van Gogh.

She reaches out to him. Brushes away auburn strands of his thinning hair. Then, one more bump. The nose-burn and tingle-eye blinking before the drip-down. "Today is a waltz," she whispers, swallowing.

Her eyes water into fuzzy blurs. They focus out-of-focus on the end of her cigarette, beyond her periphery. There, a butterfly flying outside the window, where oil and flesh upend the sky until it vomits clear, brilliant blue brushstrokes.

Fly, butterfly flying by, she thinks and smiles. Butter-flying over suburban fields, the soft green shards of manicured lawns. "You're leaving today," she says, too hot.

"I'm leaving today," he replies, too cold.

He fiddles with the white powder in the spoon. Little crystals like Gulf beach white sand clumped together in vice. He snorts the tiny piles. Tosses his head back. Feels his own drip-down.

"You're leaving," she whispers.

"Yes, I am," he says.

Cigarette smoke and imbibed libations. Liquid and crystal sins, temptations ingested. One curse for the morning brightness, another for the sounds of birds transmigrating, one for the crickets chirping. And one for the butterfly just because it's fucking morning.

"This doesn't seem like morning," she says.

"No, it doesn't," he says.

"I keep telling the sun to go down, but it won't," she says. "I want the shadows. And a fire. Let's pull the curtains."

He laughs. "Why?"

Swallowing hardest her deepest cries, she leaps at him. No hands and all mouth, she spills the drinks of their makeshift picnic. Cracks the vials of illegal pharmacy into rubble glass and powder. She falls. He topples backward and holds her steady during a barrage of kisses and tears.

"Just stay," she says. "Please."

"Please," he says. "Come."

She whispers between his words. "Stay."

He brushes her cheek with a knuckle. "Come."

Her eyes, fierce and angry and swollen and liquid-colored, fill with trembling. They water down now, drowning the both of them in wet salt. Her sometimes Baptism is lost and tired and desperate and frightened in monotones. Her eyes begin to rummage for hues.

"Stay," she says.

"It's early," he says, head in her lap.

Sight, dawn, memory. Her morning smells—honeysuckle, rainbows, earth. Her smoky-sweet breath from baby-doll lips. Her button nose, her teddy bear eyes. Her forehead, the lines, furrows and microscopic hairs there. The freckles that pop from summer tanning by the lake.

A tear falls into his mouth.

He laughs. "For someone who claims to not know music," he says, "you breathe and cry in three-four time."

"What's that?" she asks.

"A waltz," he replies.

"See?" she howls at him, pounds his chest. No thought for balance or need for control. And no explanation needed.

"What?"

"Don't leave me."

He kisses her neck. "I love you."

She bites his neck. "I hate you."

Squeezing shut his eyes precludes the sight of her. Savoring her scents, he opens his eyes and drinks her in. He drifts away and feels juicy euphoria. Leans into his own lightheadedness where strength evaporates. He remembers things, the sudden yesterday kinds of things. A flashpoint replay, his mind stretches like putty over the shortened breath of temporal absence. And somewhere in the fog, he feels her hands move from his neck to explore other regions of his geography.

He awakens, aware again.

And she suddenly knows the weight of her own tears. She weeps enough for them both. Since crawling into and out of each other's windows—all of their lives—she weeps for them both.

"I'll cry for you," she tells him.

"I am crying," he says.

"I know," she says and lowers her head. Her hair, an annoyance now, tickles his face. He pulls away—too quickly, too into his own morning. He stands, watches her sit Indian-style. He lights another cigarette.

"I have to take this first step," he says, blowing his smoke.

"Into the unknown?" she asks, spitting her fire. "It doesn't make this easier, you know. Just because you need to tame the world a little doesn't make this easier. My home is here. Your home is here."

He nods. "My home is here."

She turns away. "My home is here."

After the tempest, I am shipwrecked, she thinks. Storm and wind, and then an island—unfamiliar, dangerous, impetuous. Come unto these yellow sands, children. Take hands, children. Curtsy and take hands, and then kiss the wild waves wist.

Full-fathom five, so foot it featly.

"Somewhere else in the world," she whispers, "someone else is leaving. Someone else is leaving somewhere else at this very moment."

"Come with me," he says.

"Stay with me," she says.

She stares at him. Ages pass in brief, fiery seconds. She

adjusts the angle of her face, a solar sail to catch encroaching sunlight peeking through the window. Still smoking, he stands there. She goes to him and traces the bright paths outlining his neck and jaw and shoulder.

"I thought you didn't want light," he says.

"I don't know you in this light," she says and moves her finger down his arm. "Funny how a person can be young and old at the same time. I can see that on you now. I can feel that inside me now. That light festers in a soup of ugly truth."

She, swallowing, crashes into herself. Guilt, fury and despair take her to early memories of nameless past things. Haunted, unnamed and never-named things. The ticking away of her every-things. Her life is an antique clock that finally slows after years of ticking and tocking. Floating numbers without a face and nameless hands without direction.

Ticking, the soft scratches of rhythm grasping for questions with metronome sounds. Tocking, the beats of staccato keening cleaving those sounds with hollow answers.

Tick-tock.

Somewhere, an engine shatters and breaks the silent sky

before it plummets to the earth.

Tick-tock.

Somewhere, a steel pipe smashes into a windshield and rapes a silent car waiting for its driver.

Tick-tock.

Somewhere, a swing-set creaks from the weight of too-many children and their rambunctious friends.

Tick...

Somewhere, a dog barks.

...tock.

She slaps him. He pulls her into his body as she mumbles her stream-of-conscious madness.

"Stay," she says.

"Come," he says.

"I'll haunt you—that much I know—I'm breaking."

"You're not breaking," he whispers.

Stepping backward with a manic shudder, she recoils. "I can taste time. Time when we first held hands. When we first kissed. When we first fucked, first made love. Don't look at me like that."

He is sunlight now.

"Remember when we were eight years old?" he says. "We played around our peach tree after supper, pretending to make movies?"

"I fell on my head and blacked out."

"And when you finally woke, I was crying."

"You were crying. It's the last time I ever saw you cry."

"I thought you were dead," he says.

"It was so quiet, the way you cried," she says. "That's my most vivid memory, you know. What is it?"

He lunges for her, and they fall to their knees.

Hands knead each other's body, pulling skin, ripping off buttons. Breathing heavy, they eat one another. Teeth meet hair and flesh and lips that bleed like water. They laugh, ravenous and starving, furious and wild. Fingers on skin and creases. Pores open like hundreds of tiny greedy hungry mouths. Bone, muscle, the dried salt tracks of tears to taste—all goose-fleshed, yes. Over and over again, yes.

Then, finally, the utter silence of freedom.

One, entered and filled—the other, inside and emptied. And their echoes, like fading muted colors, become the glue of that silence. They know what it looks like. How it tastes and smells. How it creeps.

He tickles her arm. "It's time."

She heats a strange clanging as the tone changes. She moves away to dress apart from him. The sky inside blackens.

"Please, come."

"Please, stay."

"No."

"No."

Real tears are slow in coming. She watches him pack light things, the small things. Watches him take the last two bags outside. Watches as he adds them to the packed thing about to take him from her. She stares at him, finished with his pre-flight, and waits for the first of his last moves. She tries not to weep—he doesn't have to try.

They swallow melancholy and terror with smiles.

They taste their separate fates, bitter and too-spicy.

They do not say good-bye.

When she nods, he leaves her alone at the window. She watches him open his car and climb inside. Watches him close the door and start the engine. Watches him sit there and stare at the wheel, waiting for his deus ex machina.

Minutes pass—or days, she's not that certain.

But neither is he.

Frozen with hope, she searches the bones of a long-ago déjà vu memory. She remembers a gray sky, the quickness of her breathing fogging the panes of glass, the same emptiness from watching him leave.

"I was eleven," she says aloud. "Your parents were taking you to camp. You were waiting in the car. From the front porch, I waited for the car to leave the driveway. When it did, I chased after it and yelled for your father to stop. You climbed over the backseat and touched your hand to the rear window. Then, you were gone. I was screaming and running until the sting of stitches in my side stopped me."

Tick-tock.

I would have chased you forever.

Tick-tock.

Somewhere else, someone is leaving, too.

Tick-tock.

Right now, someone else is backing a car down the driveway.

Tick-tock.

Yes, someone else is leaving.

He backs the car down the driveway. Heavy with too many things, he grinds the gears. The car groans and lurches forward in fits. On impulse, she bolts outside and runs toward the vehicle. He doesn't see her. He can't see through all the baggage stacked behind him. The car finally moves onward, the sputtering engine muffling her screams.

Her voice rattles into a hoarse, soundless shout. She doesn't care how she must look, like a desperate woman, surely. She only cares about him.

And he's gone.

Yes, she is eleven all over again. That same girl is breathless all over again. The asphalt is cruel on her bare feet. There's a stitch in her side. She stops when the rear brakes of his car burn red. Her face frozen against the rising sun, she slowly trudges up the sloping street. Listens to birds. Feels the cool breezes. Her feet burn. She knows they are bleeding. A hundred more yards to go, and—

His car disappears over the other side of the hill.

Tick-tock.

She limps to the curb and collapses there. She winces and looks at her feet. Studies the spot of cement and asphalt between her legs instead. Hears the tick-tocking sounds of her mind echo. Closing her eyes, she measures the cruelty of angels with every heartbeat. He is gone now.

Tick-tock.

She vomits. An oozing wetness from inside her begins spilling into her underwear. A strange dizziness finds her and tips her face forward. Staring at the space between her bleeding feet, she sees a pool of red, the remnants of life no longer harbored inside her.

Tick-tock.

God has taken a crowbar to my womb.

She laughs. The heat of the morning sun explodes overhead. She doesn't hear the sound of a man's voice calling to her. She's too sleepy and heavy to lift her head. She closes her eyes as a pair of strong arms lift her off the hot street. She smiles. It seems all the drowsy colors of the world are gently carrying her to a place that doesn't echo as the ticking clock inside her head. There is only his voice, the only sound that matters. It is the only color worth hearing.

*

Tomorrow, Samsara

Conceptual first chapter from an unfinished sci-fi novel.

Floating in blackness, an endless dreamout.

"...gang-related uprisings increase..."

Drifting in a soup of oblivion, voices from far away.

"...due to decentralized bi-monthly inoculations..."

Memories of nothingness—a place without warmth, a limbo place where night things touched him. Those shadows were giving birth to other thoughts, other imaginings. His senses flipped and flopped into a kind of synesthesia. But even that was black and cold.

"...consolidation talks with Canada and Mexico...a unified North America...one continent, one nation..."

He was a fetus. The quickening of his heartbeat came. It tasted of hot pepper briars. It sounded of clove cigarettes. His grogginess made for an earth-brown music, like the clicking of marbles and the boiling of sweet clay. Synesthesia, yes—all senses swapped and backward now.

He heard snails moving like migratory birds across miles of his skin. The feel of their slime was akin to the strings of Vivaldi, autumn notes of butternut squash and other symphonic gourds. His chattering teeth were crystal machine guns, the taste of taupe and metal raspberries.

"...stem the tide of immigrants..."

Where in the hell am I?

A film coated his mind with uneasy white noise. There were gaps in his memory where the surreal music of lucid dreaming played.

Wasn't he only just dreaming? Weren't there gardens of butterflies and a farmhouse of people? Weren't there oceans of women glowing with unborn children? Weren't there sensations of falling and anxious waiting for inevitable things? And wasn't he in love?

Where am I?

He stirred, and that blackness turned to gray in the cold air. He felt a hand on his face, the warmth of a blanket.

"...ratified extension of congressional powers...death toll in Russia, Asia, and India 1.5 billion...Europe and United States...curbed by vaccine..."

He breathed with purpose, deeper and longer.

"...that's the news...'Flamenco Sketches' from *Kind of Blue.*"

There were scents of pine cleaner, newly washed skin, old food drying on dirty plates, the lingering odors of camphor and medicinal plastic, band-aids and gauze, and homemade bread baking. His senses were returning to normal now. He heard the beeping of machines, the pop of radio static.

It was four o'clock in the morning.

Where am I?

The language sounded alien, but as he listened, words and their meanings became clearer. Content to absorb and relearn, he kept his eyes closed and listened.

"...in local news, rioting and escalating violence in Norcross, Doraville, and Sandy Springs...skirmishes against local military and police forces. All curfews remain in effect until further notice. Due to the continued risk of contagion...the CDC and Army National Guard...deployment of more mobile vaccination units today. We will announce full schedules shortly. In world news..."

The muffled noise of distant gunfire and rocket blasts came. Sounds of warfare made him open his eyes.

But it was too damn bright to keep them completely open. He blinked often. Heavy fighting was nearby. He listened to the thumping buzz of myriad engines. Flocks of helicopters and armored vehicles moved in a parade of violence somewhere above his head. He tried his eyes again— better, but still painful. Vision was little more than a blur, but he could infer using his other heightened senses.

He felt like putty. He was on a gurney beneath a bubble of clear plastic. He wore a cotton gown. Damp earth smells told him he was underground—some secret lab or hospital room. Multicolored wires and tubes hooked him to an array of clicking and beeping machines. Lights flickered as an explosion shook the room. Alarms made his heart burst into staccato blips, and they amplified inside the reliquary of monitors at his head.

The double doors opened and a short woman with black hair and brown skin entered the room. Wearing a white lab coat and stethoscope, she wiped his face with a warm cloth and punched a nearby keyboard.

She took his temperature and blood pressure, and then gave him a few sips of ice water. The taste of his mouth demanded a strip of mint gum, but he was fine with the water. She lifted his head and told him to drink slowly.

He choked on a piece of ice.

Had we met before?

He tried asking the question, but found he couldn't speak. Again, he tried, but sounds refused to congeal into words. It was a torturous laryngitis. And then there were the pathetic croaks and grunts, and even a few monkey noises. He mouthed the words, *Do I know you?*

She shook her head. "I'm Dr. Patel," she said with a smile. "You'd be surprised. Comatose people are quite aware of their surroundings—no doubt you heard me speaking to you. Maybe you dreamed of me."

Me in a coma? And did I dream of you?

Dr. Patel's educated British-Indian accent was hypnotic. Its resonance infused her words with authority and empathy. After adjusting his blanket, she examined his eyes. "Your condition's much improved," she said, "and I'm waiting for the results of your recent bloodwork. Now that you're conscious, you'll be transfered to another facility. I wouldn't be surprised if Colonel Navarre gives you a personal escort."

Another facility—where in the hell am I now?

Again, he mouthed the question.

Dr. Patel spoke of a subsurface medical research center under midtown Atlanta, a subterranean bunker between Georgia Tech and the Varsity. The names of places sparked immediate reconnections before suddenly fading to gray. His gaze lingered on the doctor's face longer than was necessary. With a blush, he turned away.

After listening to his breathing, Dr. Patel touched the dark screen of a computer fastened to her arm. "Managing residual effects of a coma isn't easy, Mr. Larson. Do you remember why you're here? What's been happening up there? Do you remember anything at all?"

He pointed to the radio and wobbled his palm.

Dr. Patel shined a pen light into his eyes. "Today is the first day of spring," she said, casually. "I've been down here since the middle of January. It's too dangerous to be up there without a police escort. Gangs in the MARTA subway tunnels are blowing up buildings to root out drug supplies or caches of vaccine, or survivors to kill for sport—who knows? At any rate, it doesn't feel like the first day of spring, Mr. Larson."

Larson? That's not my name. I don't think.

He pantomimed writing. Dr. Patel gave him a notepad and pen. Uncertain about the mechanics, his shaky hand hovered above the paper. He took a breath and started scribbling loops, wavy lines, and odd spirals. He tossed the scrap pages to the floor. The scribbles began to resemble rudimentary letters and numbers.

Finally remembering how to put them together, he scrawled a row of fuzzy glyphs and pointed to the page.

N-A-M-E. N-O-T. L-A-R-S-O-N.

Dr. Patel tapped her arm screen. "Your chart says your name is Benjamin Francis Larson. You are twenty years-old and a freshman at UGA, and that your parents are deceased. Ring any bells?"

Deceased?

Feeling detached, he shook his head and struggled to sit upright. Dr. Patel touched his chest and gently pressed. And when she smiled, something soothed him. Her eyes and face were familiar. She smelled of sandalwood and lilacs. "What's the last thing you do remember?" she asked.

He grabbed the pad and wrote.

"Scrambled. Remember Christmas break, Mom and Dad sick. I caught what they had. Fell asleep, dreamed of end of the world, floated in darkness, heard radio. I woke up. Why can't I remember name?"

Dr. Patel listened to his heartbeat and took his pulse. "I want you to eat some solid food first—then we'll try to figure things out, okay?"

He smiled when his stomach began to rumble. After two bowls of oatmeal, a banana, a fat slice of warm bread and butter, and a glass of milk, he continued writing. Penmanship was shaky, but he formed longer sentences without pause. As his recall improved, he wrote about family. How his given name was Larson, but it wasn't the name he called himself. Memories didn't come easy, and he hit mental blocks more often than not.

Frustrated, he asked other things.

"Is the colonel a doctor too?" he wrote.

Tapping her tablet, she rolled her stool over. "A prominent neuroscientist too, but you'd never know it, not with that Southern accent of his," she said. "He knows more about neurology, biotechnology, psychiatry, and transmissible spongiform encephalopathy than most."

"Transgender spongifopoly—WTF?"

She laughed. "Please forgive me—it's been a long time since I've chatted with anybody outside of my field. TSEs are fatal degenerative brain diseases. Proteins that carry the disease make holes in the brain as it deteriorates, like a sponge. You remember mad cow disease?"

Trying to follow wasn't easy, but he managed.

He nodded that yes, he understood.

"The virus you carried is what Navarre calls a Frankenstein contagion," she said. "It spreads via air, water, body fluids, food, genes—an Alzheimer's superflu that damages like prion diseases and spreads faster than any infection in recorded history."

"Sounds like somebody was playing God," he wrote.

Dr. Patel read the words and said nothing.

"Am I still sick?" he scribbled.

It was a valid question. Dr. Patel didn't know how to answer without causing confusion or distress. She tapped her touch screen and turned around a monitor. Across the screen were paired images of what looked like pomegranate halves. "Can you see the screen?" she asked.

He nodded.

"Six days ago, you arrived here infected and in a coma," she said, tapping and pointing. "You lingered in an REM-like state for five days totally asymptomatic—aside from the coma. These scans of your brain indicate no holes, even though the virus was in your system. Yesterday, your hippocampus and neocortex became hypersynaptic. Memory, language, consciousness, other higher brain functions—all are rooted there. These scans here show the activity of a brain free from degenerative tissue damage."

"What does that mean, Dr. Patel?"

"That you are apparently immune to a virus that's killed

almost half the world's population. The impaired motor skills, the dissociation, the memory loss—all are temporary."

"And there's a vaccine?"

Lifting her hair, she exposed the back of her neck. "Yes, a painful one shot directly into the spinal chord," she said. "We need an injection every two weeks because—he's here."

They both looked up. A helicopter landed on the surface above their heads. Sounds of thumping faded as its spinning engine eased. A disembodied voice on the intercom announced the guests. From the far end of the corridor came the hard cadence of marching feet—five or six pairs coming fast. Two pairs faded down an intersecting hallway, their heavy echoes out of step with the others still coming closer.

Dr. Patel pulled the plastic sheet from the metal hoop overhead and cleared stray wires and unnecessary tubes. Glancing at the doors, she gazed at her patient. "There are rumors," she said, straightening his sheets. "You dreamed the virus away."

Dreamed the virus away?

Before he could respond, three men in fatigues and armadillo-gray body armor entered the room. Two younger soldiers stood sentry at the doors.

The older one moved ahead with a duffle bag and a manila envelope. Keeping his attention on the young man, he greeted them both with a curt nod. At the foot of the bed, he tossed the envelope and dumped the bag's contents, gray fatigues and two white lab coats.

"Good morning, Colonel Navarre."

"G'Morning, Patel," he drawled. "Sorry for the short notice, but I'm closing this facility. The patient will require a physician, so I've arranged for you to depart with him. Pack this bag with enough supplies for several days and any personal effects if there's space left."

"What about the data?"

"Ah, yes," Navarre said. "Your touch tablet, my dear."

A bewildered Dr. Patel removed the computer from her arm. The colonel tapped a few keys. "You've entered all the data, correct?" he asked as he tapped the screen again. "I'll be upset if you haven't."

"Yes, sir," she replied. "All data about the young man, Colonel—"

He raised a hand. When he finished tapping, he smashed

the small computer on the floor. It sparked, smoked, and hissed. "My dear, this young man and I are gonna talk," said Navarre. "Soldiers, you have orders."

They shouted, "Yes, sir."

As Dr. Patel followed the men from the room, distant gunfire made for a perfectly surreal soundtrack. Sounds of exploding weaponry on the surface penetrated through the corridors deep below, masking all activity in the labs and offices. Battle noise reverberated throughout the facility.

The colonel sat in the vacated stool. He wore his uniform well, cutting an impeccable, imposing figure of a man. He smelled of Old Spice.

"I'm John Navarre," he said. "We've met before, son, so don't worry about the memory glitch. Your brain's rebooting—I'm just helping it along before you and Patel leave. You'll be sick as a dog until your equilibrium readjusts, but it'll pass in a couple of days. I don't have time to pussyfoot, so I'll be blunt: a few pissant politicians would rather you not exist. They say you're a threat to national security—yes, you. At this very moment, these ass-clowns are debating what is to be done with you. Before the sons of bitches convene their committee and order a bullet served with your afternoon ham sandwich, I'm getting you out of here."

There was regret in the colonel's eyes—and anger.

"This global catastrophe kept me up at night long before you walked into my life," he said, "but after you did, I haven't slept at all. You told me that you dreamed the virus away. That you had visions about what might help us stop the spread of it. We were desperate for any possible solution. Despite our doubts, you let us study you. You told us what proteins to block and in what order, which led us to a vaccine. Since your government refuses to keep a promise, I will—here, give me that pen and pad."

Visions, visions of what?

There was an explosion overhead. Under the dusty rain of ceiling debris, he felt nothing but the weight of much heavier things. Somehow, he knew this Colonel John Navarre, and volunteering for weird experiments, and even now, they felt like dreams.

But I remember...

"When you first woke up in a fugue-like amnesia," Navarre said, scribbling, "you told me to say this word. I don't understand how it works, but you said it would. It's the name you can't remember."

Navarre whispered the name into his ear.

Something inside him tingled. Letters clicked into place like tumblers. Pulses of electricity moved under hairless skin. He scratched head and the baldness was familiar. His arms and his legs, his face, his eyebrow ridges—and then he remembered more.

My name...

He remembered another time of discovery: a time of perceiving things differently, a time of seeing connections between problems and solutions, a time of knowing that nothing imagined was impossible.

My name...

Other memories, smaller ones about his parents and larger ones about his life with them, swiveled into view. How his father had been a man of spirit and machines. How he'd believed that a man's power lay in the deep roots of calloused hands. How his mother had been a woman of vision and violent imagination. How she'd believed that any magic still left in the world was merely tucked away and sleeping. And he'd buried them side by side under a peach tree. He'd dug the graves just before the virus took him.

He looked at Navarre and smiled—*I know my name.*

"My name is Fable," he said. "I remember now."

"Easy, son," said Navarre. "How do you feel?"

"Like shit—God Almighty, I was trapped in here."

Navarre laughed. "Any new visions, son?"

"Yes, but they're fuzzy, and I'm still not—"

Another explosion rocked the room. Feeling dizzy, Fable vomited into his blanket and fought the earlier darkness. The rush of returning memories, the accumulation of experiences he'd forgotten, the new details of emotions and thoughts—they overwhelmed and weakened him. He threw up again and tried not to slip away.

He blacked out. And then he woke up to arguing voices.

"...have you done?"

"...your only concern...him to safety, Patel."

"...what did you say to him that..."

"...I need him alive...you keep him that way..."

Fable opened his eyes.

Dr. Patel was there wiping his face and removing the

soiled blanket. She must have seen him faint on the monitor. "Don't try to talk," she said. "Here, let me see that— Colonel, do you know about his hand?"

Navarre was speaking into a device at his wrist. He nodded for Dr. Patel to examine it herself. She looked at Fable's palm. A ring of pale light began to glow in the center.

Pressing there, its skin became a transparent membrane. Clearly seen beneath it were ligaments, tendons, and muscles as he wiggled his fingers. "Colonel, would you mind telling me about this?" she asked, her voice quavering. "Why is his hand doing this? What did your team do?"

"Patel, I'm leaving that to you," he said. "This young man faced the worst plague in human history and made himself immune to the goddamned thing. It's your job to figure out why and how. You have a year to learn all you can before I come looking for you. Consider our debt settled, young man. You've work ahead of you, and come next spring, any meeting between yours and mine will be strictly protocol."

"Dammit, Navarre, what you did to this kid?"

Navarre said, "He'll tell you when he remembers. And I

didn't do anything to him that he didn't volunteer to have done. I owe him for that."

The main generator exploded and part of the ceiling collapsed. A panicked voice on the intercom announced the evacuation of the facility and ordered any remaining personnel to leave immediately. Lights flickered as the loudspeaker crackled to dead air.

The back-up generator exploded, shutting off all active systems and plunging the room into darkness.

Navarre opened the envelope and directed his flashlight over its spilled contents. "Looks like we're outta time," he said. "Wear those fatigues and coats and take the service tunnel behind you to the next one. Wait at the entrance. When the stopwatch sounds its alarm, cross the causeway to the lower parking deck of the Bank of America building. This key is for the black armor-plated SUV there. This map will take you out of the city. These badges will get you through all checkpoints within a 75-mile radius for three days. You have until 0500 to be as far from here as possible."

At Navarre's wrist, a voice barked an incoherent phrase. As a helicopter's engine began whirring on the surface, he responded in military speak before returning his attention to Fable. There was something final about the departure. Lines were drawn, sides were taken, and they both knew it.

"Thank you, Colonel," said Fable, extending his hand.

Navarre shook it. "Throwing out baby and bathwater isn't what's best for the country," he said. "Never doubt that I won't know where you are or what you're doing—until next spring, you're on borrowed time."

And then Colonel John Navarre departed.

Dr. Patel secured their supplies and the envelope's contents. She dressed Fable and herself. She pushed him down the service tunnel in a wheelchair, stopping short of the entrance to the second tunnel. They waited for the alarm. Aside from sounds of escalating street fighting, it was utterly silent in the corridor.

If it hadn't been for the strange steady glow of Fable's hand, it would have been too dark to see. Dr. Patel kept her gaze fixed to the floor. "I can't deny this is extraordinary," she said. "Did you really dream away the virus?"

"Yes, I believe I did," he said.

"Can you show me how to do it?"

"Yes, I can—it's not all that hard."

She pointed to his hand. "And that? Did you do that?"

Fable held it up. "Yes, I did."

Explosions and shaking sent down ceiling tiles.

"After my parents died, I volunteered to be re-infected with new strains of the virus," he said. "At first, I'd wake up in a fugue state with a glowing hand and a body free from infection. I started having visions after they developed the vaccine. Navarre ordered the studies stopped, but Surgeon General Lewis rescinded the order."

Several F-35 Lightning strikers flew overhead.

"Visions? What kind?"

Fable took her hand. "After your cancer went into remission, doctors said you couldn't have children. Your grandfather visited you in a dream and told you that they were wrong. Your family disowned you because you married your husband here instead of India. You've not seen them since. Your husband died three years ago in a car accident, but you didn't keep his last name. But you have another name too."

Two large blasts shook the tunnel.

Patel could barely speak. "I've never told anyone."

"Your grandfather called you by that name."

"Don't," she pleaded. "It's the name of an exiled woman."

"It's a sacred name."

"It's my karma today, and then tomorrow, samsara— I've spent my life away from superstition. Please stop. How can you know this?" Dr. Patel squeezed his hand and grimaced. "Why is your hand so hot?"

Fable doubled over. "Something's wrong. We need to go—"

A mortar hit the north end of the facility. Cracked open from the surface to the floors underground, exposed for anyone to ransack. There were sounds of people running through empty hallways, back and forth between the offices and labs. Firing weapons filled the air, obscenities and screaming. Another blast brought more sounds of gunfire.

The stopwatch sounded its alarm—*beep, beep, beep!*

There was a high-pitched screech of an incoming rocket just before its explosion tore open the second tunnel.

Smoke filled the service corridor as five armed men fell scrambled into the new opening.

Adjusting his visor, a sixth stumbled ahead and shouted,

"There's two up here—fucking kill 'em if they don't got the goddamn vaccine. Grab the woman first, boys!"

...beep...

All six men fell on them. Taking Dr. Patel, they jabbed her with fingers and the butts of their weapons, ripping her clothes. They toppled over the wheelchair and kicked at Fable, trapped in its seat and convulsing.

...beep, beep...

When he opened his eyes, the seizure ended. His fist grew brighter and hotter. He opened his hand and released a beam of white from its center. Horror-stricken and paralyzed, the six invaders stood helpless as the light penetrated their bodies and cooked them from the inside out. It vaporized them into piles of bones, clouds of dust and sulfur. The haunted, reeking air was ripe with the scent of overcooked meat. The added stench of human waste prompted coughing from the two survivors.

...beep, beep, beep!

The stopwatch alarm abruptly ended.

One minute had passed into the strangest silence. More jets screamed overhead. Fable moaned. Dr. Patel moved through debris to pull his wheelchair upright. She checked his pulse and breathing, secured their supplies, and then pushed him toward the opening of the second tunnel. Up a smashed concrete ramp and down another, she pushed him to the opposite end of the causeway.

"Talk to me," she said. "Stay with me."

Dizzy and nauseous, Fable murmured a response.

Stopping in the lower parking deck to check his vitals, Dr. Patel mopped the stream of blood pouring from his head. "Stay with me."

"Not going anywhere," he said. "You'll have to drive though."

She laughed. "That's not funny."

"Get me into the SUV," he said. "I need to sleep."

"Fable, please."

It was the first time that she'd used the name.

"I'm not hurt," he said. "I'm just tired, Sita. You have the most beautiful hair. Did you know that?"

She wiped a tear. "What did you call me?"

Fable smiled. "Sita, the name your grandfather called you." And then he fell into the void.

He tumbled and swam, and then he floated there.

Thoughts the mass of planets ignited the star engine in his mind. Its gravity arrested him as he witnessed himself giving birth to himself.

He understood the vast distances between atoms. That the stuff of stars is the stuff of souls. That a sacred name burns so bright in the mind that it shines its light on the darkest roads. That futures are only single moments of time stretched to hell and back like vicious orbs of déjà vu.

How long he was under Fable didn't know.

He knew she was weeping as they were leaving the garage. He felt the rumble of the engine, the smooth glide over paved city streets. He whispered her name—sometimes as a chant, sometimes as a prayer—and he knew what he'd say to her when he woke and they were safe.

Sita held his hand as he slept.

Fable saw nothing but bright sunlight as he dreamed. And it was the sweetest peace he'd ever known.

*

D. B. Patterson

The Wish

A chilling tale written for this collection.

My brother calls me Killer.

He has since the night Mom and Dad died. Even though my sole responsibility these past few years has been to care for my quadriplegic little brother, he nonetheless delights in calling me Killer. I can count on one hand the number of times that he's called me anything but Killer (asshole doesn't count). The point is that he never uses my given name anymore, and I wish he would.

Whether to summon or damn me, praise or accuse me, I miss hearing it spoken aloud. I miss hearing it echo inside my head. I miss feeling it resonate inside my heart.

Sometimes, I really do wish that.

Sometimes—there's a dangerous word.

A seemingly benign adverb that has the ability to become malignant with the violence of literal truth. But then, who am I to mince a weak word's wonky wobble? I know what I mean whenever I say that sometimes I wish my brother wouldn't call me Killer. I know what I've done. Even if he started calling me Sweet Baby James (not my real name), it wouldn't alter the trajectory of our conjoined fates, recalibrate the influence of our unlucky stars, or resurrect our dead parents and my fiancé.

Nothing would change, not even sometimes. All I can do is accept my lot and cherish the daily hour of solitude I get each morning. I look forward to it every goddamn day, rain or shine.

I wake before the sunrise. I lie in my bed and stare at the ceiling in the cool hue of pre-dawn. I take long deep breaths and imagine a Walter Mitty-esque fantasy escape for a moment or two. I never linger there, nor do I go back to sleep. I never waste the brief time I have.

This morning is no different.

I wake up before my alarm sounds. I get out of bed to relieve myself. I wash my hands and face, scrub the funk off my teeth with a quick brush and gargle. I fumble with my running shorts and shoes (laid out the night before) as I simultaneously stretch on my bedroom floor. And then I'm out the door for a run on the beach.

It's how my mornings have started for nearly four years. A routine that has kept me sane. Well, that coupled with the knowledge that my prison term ends tomorrow. Tomorrow, I am longer bound to my brother. Mom and Dad's will stipulated four years was all that was required of me before I could take my half of the trust to start a new life.

What my brother does with his share isn't my business.

Today, I'm up earlier than usual—go figure. The morning is brisk. It's foggy too—the stuff is just rolling in off the ocean. No matter—as soon as the sun breaks the horizon, warmer winds and clearer skies will come. All around me, the sounds of waves crashing, seashells crunching, seagulls laughing, and crabs clicking.

Joy to the world, bitches—let heaven and nature sing.

Aside from changes in the weather, my mornings have rarely varied. Oh, the distance between the house and my point of turning back north of it has lengthened. My endurance and strength have improved. My overall well-being is beyond measure. There's always been a sweet continuity to my slow, methodical improvement.

This is the thought I ponder as I approach the jetty before the old lighthouse, which I can barely see. It isn't in service, but a spindly old tower looming high above a scenic beach makes for a rather imposing sight, fog or no.

I've seen the same spire nearly every day for the past four years too—a dim distant beacon beckoning me ever closer.

Now that I'm here it *feels* like a bad omen.

Its shadowy outline reminds me to turn back. But when the fog vanishes, as a gray veil lifted by unseen hands, the lighthouse is suddenly awash with clarity. For a moment, I imagine myself keeping watch there.

As I jog in place, I entertain the idea of a spontaneous expedition too. It's just a hundred or so yards away.

So what if I'll be late—who cares?

Rhetorical question.

If I go exploring, I know how the rest of my day will unfold. Upon my late return, I'll find my brother waiting for me in the kitchen. He'll offer nothing but an icy stare as I drink my glass of orange juice.

After basking in the desert glare of his enmity, I'll change his soiled clothes—he shits himself when he's pissed at me. I'll serve breakfast in the nook overlooking the ocean, but he'll spit out most of the meal. If I don't have to change him again, I'll wheel him around the house our parents left us. And for an hour or so, I'll listen to him swear at me and curse his stars.

No, I can't be late.

I don't want to make our last day miserable simply because I explored the lighthouse for ten minutes. Tomorrow will be here soon enough. Besides, the fog is rolling in again.

Shaking my head, I make my way back home.

My hour of freedom done for the day, I find myself standing on the beach looking at the house, the waves crashing behind me. I feel a lump of thick dread in my throat as I approach the wraparound porch.

My hand freezes on the doorknob. I bid farewell to the

sunrise. My only thought is on tomorrow. By this time to-morrow, Ben will no longer be my responsibility. And I will no longer be his punching bag. Until then, I will take care of him, as I have done.

I take a deep breath and pray.

Dear God, let tomorrow finally be the end to this hell.

Heaving a sigh, I enter the house. My brother is waiting for me in the dark kitchen. He sits in his wheelchair like an egg rotting from the inside out. He nods to his lap. "This is addressed to you. Someone slipped it through the mail slot, rang the doorbell, and left."

"Envelope? From who?"

His face twists into a sneer. "If you'd been here on time, you'd know."

The scent of shit fills my nostrils. The manila envelope in his lap casts an upward glow under his pale chin, a hair-less beard of defused yolk. "Open it, idiot," he spits, roll-ing the joystick control of his chair in his fingers. The pro-truding rig careens into my shin—not the first time either. He smiles at me with icy eyes. "Oops," he says, spinning around. "Why are you getting mail so early? Are you keeping secrets from me?"

"No, Ben—and I wasn't expecting anything."

"Stop lying, Killer."

"I'm not lying."

"Then open it in front of me!"

Ben's chest rises and falls. He cowers as my hand nears his lap. The marigold-hued envelope is clasped, not licked. It feels empty. I don't recognize the handwriting of my name scribbled on its front. It looks like chicken scratch.

"Open it," Ben shrieks. "What's inside? What is it?"

"A diamond chip and a note," I reply, reading the note in silence as I wipe a stream of sweat. "I wonder who left this."

Ben coughs. "Like I fucking know your friends."

"I have no friends, little brother—just you."

"Nobody likes an asshole, Killer."

I offer him a weak smile. "You didn't see who left it?"

Ben looks down. "No, I didn't," he says. "By the time I got to the door, nobody was there. I accidentally broke the mail basket."

"I bet."

"I'm hungry. Feed me."

"I need to clean you first," I tell him.

"Fuck you," he shouts. "I hate it when you leave. I hate being alone."

"I know, Ben, and I'm sorry I was a few minutes late," I tell him gently. "I promise, it won't happen again."

"Fuck you, Killer. What does the note say?"

"It says, 'One wish, a stone's kiss to find your bliss.'"

"Find your bliss?"

"Find your bliss," I repeat. "I can barely read the writing."

"Find *your* bliss, Killer," he says with a sneer. "Maybe that's your way out, big brother. Make a wish, find your bliss. Far away from me."

"You read my mind," I say flippantly. "Must be my bliss."

"How much do you hate me?" he asks.

We stare each other down. Before I avert my eyes, I answer the question in my mind—I don't love him, but I don't hate him either. I pity him.

I mean, I'm the older brother who never got sick, never had trouble with sports or friends or girls. My little brother was always sick, always on the slow side of growth, always a sore loser and worse winner. He rarely had friends even before our parents died. And he made certain I wouldn't want to be one after I started to care for him. He knew I had to forsake my world to live with him in his—he's learned to hate me for it.

Tomorrow, he'll hate me more.

Turning away, I await the next epithet. It doesn't come. I wish it would—continuity is important. Laughing to myself, I put the note and diamond chip—a piece of junk shop plastic paste—back inside the envelope."I bet it's a direct marketing gimmick for a new jewelry store. Or a joke."

"What if it's not a joke, Killer?"

"You think it's an ad?"

Ben frowns. "What if it is what it says it is?"

"A real wish, you mean? Oh, come on—that's silly."

"What if it wasn't? What would you wish for?"

I slide it across the countertop like a Frisbee. "I don't know—let's talk about it after I clean you up. I'm sorry I wasn't here when it arrived."

"No, you're not."

Closing my eyes, I count to ten. Slowly. "What do you want me to do, Ben? I can't go back in time to be ON time.

I can't go back in time to stop the crash. I can only be here in the present, Ben—today, right now."

"Until t-t-t-tomorrow," my brother stammers.

Until tomorrow?

He doesn't know anything about tomorrow.

Ben's speech tends to trip over his thoughts when he's lying or fear weasels into his brain, or if he feels cornered. Ignoring his blathering, I lift his from his chair, carry him to the bathroom, and drop him into the tub. While he soaks I toss his soiled clothes into the washing machine. I wipe his chair, drop him back in his seat wearing clean clothes, and wheel him around to the kitchen nook.

He keeps his mouth shut as I prepare his breakfast.

My guilt is coming at me now—does he know? No, he can't possibly know he's heading to a new group home tomorrow. He doesn't know I'm leaving tomorrow. I wonder. Would it have made a difference if he did know? Would he have been nicer to me? Would I have stayed?

I wonder.

Ben waits patiently in silence as he watches me. He doesn't complain about the food today. He seems almost grateful. The bacon and eggs, the buttered toast slices, the chunks of inch-thick melon. He can't speak when he eats—he could choke.

Normally, he eats quickly so that he can start back up again, but now he seems to be savoring the food. As he chews his last bite, his eyes dart to the countertop.

Where the envelope sits. I quickly finish my plate, and as I clear the table, Ben looks as me with tears in his eyes. "This won't sit in my stomach long," he says, limply.

"It's okay, Ben—that's why I'm here." At this, I bend over him and lightly squeeze his shoulder. "So how about stop being such a prick to me? Is that so much to ask?"

"Fuck off," he says as I wipe his wet cheeks.

Yes, it's tragically pathetic. We both know his body will reject the food soon. A glass of beet juice will be forthcoming after I clean and change his diaper again. I really shouldn't make him such a heavy breakfast—his digestive system is sensitive—but it makes him feel normal for a few minutes. I feel for Ben. I do. And I don't mind cleaning the shit out from between his legs—after four years, I don't think about it anymore.

We keep his privates shaved anyway—hairless skin makes cleaning shit a breeze. An old hospice nurse told me that trick when I first started. Ben agreed to it only if I wasn't the one doing the shaving. And so, for the past four years, a talented buxom beauty by the name of Miss Kitty calls twice a week to take care of my brother's nethers.

I'd be lying if I said that she never takes care of mine.

As I finish wiping down the table, I grab the envelope and sit beside my brother. His crying has stopped. His eyes are closed. He swallows and speaks.

"I hate you. I've always hated you."

"I know, and it's okay."

"If I could have a wish, I'd wish you were in my place," he whispers, suddenly glaring at me with red eyes. Again, I wipe his face with a clean napkin. He spits on my hand as I pull away. "I hate you."

Miss Kitty was here yesterday, but maybe she has an opening in her schedule today. I might need her to stop by. Wiping my hand, I look at Ben and ask, "Is that really what you'd wish for if that stupid diamond was real?"

He doesn't hesitate. "A thousand times, yes. Killer."

"You wouldn't wish for our parents to be alive again? Or for you to be whole again? Healthy, able to walk and care for yourself? To run and fuck? To be free from that chair?"

"No," Ben says. "I'd wish you were me and I was you."

"Lucky me."

"Yes, you are, and I hate you for it."

Standing up, I give his shoulder a squeeze. I know he despises my touch, but I do it anyway.

"Good thing I'm leaving tomorrow then," I tell him, angrily grabbing the envelope before I head outside.

I can hear him screaming that he's known all along I wouldn't stay. Of course, I ignore him as I slam the screen door and go find my little spot in the dunes.

Guilt pulls me to the sand. I hold the envelope between my finger and thumb at the corner. It swings back and forth like a pendulum—tick-tock. I watch the motion of my own swinging rectangular clock. Ben was bitter when he came screaming into the world.

This is his handwriting, I'd bet.

In fact, I wouldn't be surprised if he had more mobility than he lets on. I bet he's been hiding it from me. I certainly wouldn't put it past him, the son-of-a-bitch. It would be just like him too. He's done some fucked up shit out of desperation, so this would be par for the course.

I think of the car crash that claimed the lives of our parents. I think of the night that changed our lives. A family dinner with my fiancé. My parents too drunk to drive. My stubborn father demanding to get behind the wheel, and there's me taking the keys because I'm the responsible one.

"Give me the keys, Dad," I told him.

Give me the keys. The last words I ever said to him. I didn't have a single drink that night, and they all died anyway. Things might've been different had I let Dad drive us home. He was a better driver when he wasn't sober anyway. I knew this. He knew this. My mother and brother knew this. My fiancée Jill didn't need to know that ugly truth yet.

I lost everything when that truck plowed into us.

Miraculously, I was thrown from the car with only a cut on my forehead and a bruise under my left eye. Poor Ben was thrown from the car too, but he landed head-first twisted up like a pretzel as soon as he hit the asphalt. If wishes were possible, then I'd wish to fix that night.

If wishes were real, that is.

The back-and-forth pendulum motion of the envelope between my pinched fingers is rather hypnotic. If only this were real, if only this were real. I stop the swinging and open the goddamn envelope again.

I look at the diamond chip in my palm.

I'd wish for my brother to be whole, healthy, and happy. Like he was the summer before the car crash. It was the only time Ben genuinely seemed to be happy. We got along. We went running together. We went on double dates.

My heart leaps at the thought of him being happy again. It couldn't hurt to wish that for my brother. I decide to tell him my wish before I leave tomorrow. It's what he's wanted all along, to know how I feel.

Laughing, go back to the house, tossing the note into the bushes as I walk up the porch steps. I look at the diamond chip. One little wish. I don't know what to expect when I go to the house, but I'm hopeful.

Maybe I'll see contrition, or maybe I'll see him smile.

"Killer, what are you doing? You've been standing there for five minutes," he says, his voice breaking. "So, why don't you get it over with? I mean, you're leaving, so why wait, Killer? I'm gonna live in a group home and you'll disappear with your half of Mom and Dad's money. You kill our parents, you kill your future wife, you cripple me, and you ride off like a cowboy into the sunset. Have you no shame?"

He's the same as he ever was.

As he's always been.

As he always ever shall be.

Forgetting reality, I race to his side. He is weeping openly again. Racking, heaving sobs. And he tells me how much he despises me. How much he hates me. How unfair it is that he's not like me.

"I hate you," he says.

"I know, Ben, and I'm sorry."

"Wish me well. Do it."

"Ben," I say, looking into my palm. "If I could make a wish, I'd wish for you to be happy and—"

My brother's face becomes twisted, splotchy with mucus and spittle, and venom. "You selfish, murdering fuck," he hisses, spitting at me. "If I could, I'd wish that you had died in childbirth. I'd wish to be an only child."

"Ben, please."

"Three people would be alive had it not been for you."

"Ben, please."

"I'd be walking," he says. "I'd be whole. I'd be free."

"Ben," I say, my anger rising. "You don't mean this."

"I hate you!"

"No, you don't."

"Wish for me to be well," he says, tears spilling. "Wish for me to be healthy and strong, Killer! I can't kill you as long as I'm a cripple!"

Four years suddenly smash into my head. That night was not my fault. I killed no one. I lost everyone. But suddenly, I forget myself. My sanity, my thread of regret, my love for a brother I refused to give up on. Spiteful ink wells up inside my heart and colors the chambers black. My insides feel like smog, like sublime darkness. I feel primeval. I can't stop myself before it comes out. I can't stop the words.

"Ben, you know, sometimes," I whisper, another voice channeling my black mind. "Sometimes..."

"Sometimes, WHAT, Killer?"

"Sometimes, I wish you'd fucking die."

Ben's seething, sloppy weeping immediately ceases. A dark shadow of worry crosses his face, smoothing the wrinkles of his brow and the tiny frown lines around his mouth.

When the color rushes from his cheeks and forehead, I realize the chance to free us both has passed into oblivion. That chance was as gone from the world as the name from my old life. My brother was right to call me Killer.

"I'm sorry, Ben," I say, as his heads fall to his chest.

His final breath of air, his last heartbeat, and then he is gone. Once again, I have claimed another life. Fumbling toward his wheelchair, I grab wrist—no pulse. I place my fingers on his neck—again, no pulse. Pulling his tiny, frail body out of the seat, I slide him across the table on his back and give him mouth to mouth.

I pump his chest.

I breathe air into his lungs. I pump his chest. Minutes pass as hours. I place his body back in the chair and sit beside him. Holding his hand, I spend the rest of my morning studying Ben's fixed, glassy stare. His face is gray and his skin is cold.

By the time I'm ready to make all the necessary calls, including the one to his new group home—Yeah, thank you for keeping his space reserved. It was, yes—quite sudden and most unexpected.

No, I won't need a service to come for his body—I've pre-arranged that already, but thanks for the offer.

In my mind, as I continue to stare at my lifeless brother, I have similar conversations with other officials. That Ben shuffled off this mortal coil instantly was the only thing I knew. That's the truth of the matter, but I decide to keep the bit about making that wish to myself.

I mean, what's the point? It's not like Ben was in the best of health. Sudden death was simply the result of the paralysis and persistent stresses to his broken body. That my wish came true is merely coincidence.

A fucking coincidence!

I begin to laugh. And I can't stop laughing—*yes, Officer Charles, I wished him dead on-a accident, but I swear, sir, it won't happen again.*

This is all in my head.

Years of living in this very specific hell have taken its toll. That's all.

Reaching for the phone on the counter, I hear a sharp intake of breath behind me. I turn around and watch in horror as my dead brother sits upright in his wheelchair.

As my dead brother starts heaving gurgling breaths. A labor of breathing not unlike that of a boy drowning in a pool of shallow water. Ben moans as his breathing calms and the color returns to his face. His head lolls over to look at me. "What have you done?"

My knees buckle.

"What have you done?" he screams. "What is this?"

Rushing to his side, I grab his hand. Its warmth assuaging all shock as my sense of touch confirms to me that his death was a lie. Somehow. I don't know how long we sat there looking at each other as I held his hand. All I know is what had happened before happens again.

His death happens again.

Ben dies again.

As I'm kneeling beside him holding his hand, I can feel the warmth of his blood turning to ice. I see the pallor of his face turn from peach to bluish to gray ash to white.

No pulse. Again.

I must be losing my mind. Ben is dead again.

No, I must be hallucinating. How is this possible? Why is this happening? Letting go his hand, I fight back the tears burning my eyes and face. But when I sit beside him, I let go and sob for an hour. In fact, I cry myself to sleep. I wake to a setting sun's last light warming my face.

And then I hear the sound of my brother's voice.

Sitting up on my knees, I take his hand and feel his warmth and his color return. His head lifting slowly from his chest, Ben shifts his face toward mine. After his struggle for breath, he settles back and smiles.

"I'm so glad you're here," he says. "I had the most horrible dream."

"Dream?"

"Yes, a horrible dream," he whispers, closing his eyes. "You made a wish."

"What did I wish?"

Ben's eyes fly open. "What have you done to me?"

I don't know what to say. I don't fully understand what it is I'm seeing. Ben tries to shout again, but then, as before, all his color leaves his face as he slumps over in his chair.

Once more, I am greeted with eerie silence. And then, once again, his life returns.

But then, almost immediately after, his life passes.

That's when I realize, to my horror, what I have done. The diamond chip in my palm is gone. In its place is a tiny black hole where the words of my wish linger like waves of sound inside an echo chamber of hell.

As I stare at my hand, my brother stirs to life again. The same gasping struggle for breath, the same painful rebirth.

But this time, he lives for three days.

Until he dies once again.

He comes back to life a day later, and remains alive for two weeks. And we begin to think that maybe the time of life will lengthen after each death.

After a month of no endings, the repetitive sameness of life and death starts over again. And then again.

The absolute truth of my words was the key to the wish. I'd wished for my brother's death, yes, but only sometimes.

Just sometimes.

*

D. B. Patterson

ABOUT THE AUTHOR

D. B. Patterson writes fiction for adults, teens and kids. Patterson's short works have been published in *Elephants & Other Gods, Ramble Underground, Shalla Magazine, Larks Fiction Magazine, The Artisan, Cerulean Rain*, and others. His first novel, *Perdido River Bastard*, was published in August 2014. His books for young readers include *The Christmas Witchling* and *Little Tiger and the Year of the Dragon* adventure series. His books for early readers include four illustrated Lamby Lambpants storybook adventures and a coloring book. This is his first anthology of short stories.

Patterson is also a songwriter, vocal and artistic mechanic, classically-trained actor, digital media developer, illustrator, founder of a toy company, and a 1st Runner-up National Karaoke Champion (don't tell anyone). He is married and lives in Tarpon Springs, Florida, with his wife, Tina.

Facebook.com/dbpatterson.author.

Printed in the United States of America.
First Printing (eBook), 2014. Second Printing, 2015.

ISBN 978-0692420911

DBP PRESS
Post Office Box 399 | Tarpon Springs, FL 34688